Uncle Petros and Goldbach's Conjecture

Uncle Petros and Goldbach's Conjecture

APOSTOLOS DOXIADIS

BLOOMSBURY

First published in Greek
by Kastioniotis Editions as
O Theios Petros kai i Eikasia tou Golbach

Copyright © 1992, 2000 by Apostolos Doxiadis

Published by Bloomsbury USA, New York and London

ISBN 1-58234-067-6

10 9 8 7 6 5 4 3 2 1

CIP information available upon request

Printed in the United States of America
by R. R. Donnelley & Sons Company,
Harrisonburg, Virginia

Archimedes will be remembered when Aeschylus
is forgotten, because languages die and mathematical
ideas do not. 'Immortality' may be a silly word,
but probably a mathematician has the best
chance of whatever it may mean.

G. H. HARDY, *A Mathematician's Apology*

Uncle Petros and
Goldbach's Conjecture

One

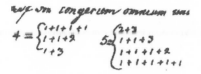

Every family has its black sheep – in ours it was Uncle Petros.

My father and Uncle Anargyros, his two younger brothers, made sure that my cousins and I should inherit their opinion of him unchallenged.

'That no-good brother of mine, Petros, is one of life's failures,' my father would say at every opportunity. And Uncle Anargyros, during the family get-togethers from which Uncle Petros routinely absented himself, always accompanied mention of his name with snorts and grimaces expressing disapproval, disdain or simple resignation, depending on his mood.

However, I must say this for them: both brothers treated him with scrupulous fairness in financial matters. Despite the fact that he never shared even a slight part of the labour and the responsibilities involved in running the factory that the three inherited jointly from my grandfather, Father and Uncle Anargyros unfailingly paid Uncle Petros his share of the profits.

(This was due to a strong sense of family, another common legacy.) As for Uncle Petros, he repaid them in the same measure. Not having had a family of his own, upon his death he left us, his nephews, the children of his magnanimous brothers, the fortune that had been multiplying in his bank account practically untouched in its entirety.

Specifically to me, his 'most favoured of nephews' (his own words), he additionally bequeathed his huge library which I, in turn, donated to the Hellenic Mathematical Society. For myself I retained only two of its items, volume seventeen of Leonard Euler's *Opera Omnia* and issue number thirty-eight of the German scientific journal *Monatshefte für Mathematik und Physik*. These humble memorabilia were symbolic, as they defined the boundaries of Uncle Petros' essential life-story. Its starting-point is in a letter written in 1742, contained in the former, wherein the minor mathematician Christian Goldbach brings to the attention of the great Euler a certain arithmetical observation. And its termination, so to speak, is to be found in pages 183–98 of the erudite Germanic journal, in a study entitled 'On Formally Undecidable Propositions in *Principia Mathematica* and Related Systems', authored in 1931 by the until then totally unknown Viennese mathematician Kurt Gödel.

*

Until I reached mid-adolescence I would see Uncle Petros only once a year, during the ritual visit on his name day, the feast of Saints Peter and Paul on the twenty-ninth of June. The custom of this annual meeting had been initiated by my grandfather and as a consequence had become an inviolable obligation in our tradition-ridden family. We journeyed to Ekali, a suburb of Athens today but in those days more of an isolated sylvan hamlet, where Uncle Petros lived alone in a small house surrounded by a large garden and orchard.

The contemptuous dismissal of their older brother by Father and Uncle Anargyros had puzzled me from my earliest years and had gradually become for me a veritable mystery. The discrepancy between the picture they painted of him and the impression I formed through our scant personal contact was so glaring that even an immature mind like mine was compelled to wonder.

In vain did I observe Uncle Petros during our annual visit, seeking in his appearance or behaviour signs of dissoluteness, indolence or other characteristics of the reprobate. On the contrary, any comparison weighed unquestionably in his favour: the younger brothers were short-tempered and often outright rude in their dealings with people while Uncle Petros was tactful and considerate, his deep-set blue eyes always kindling with kindness. They were both heavy drinkers and smokers; he drank nothing stronger than water and inhaled only the scented air of his garden. Furthermore, unlike Father, who was portly, and Uncle Anargyros, who was outright obese, Petros had the healthy wiriness resulting from a physically active and abstemious lifestyle.

My curiosity increased with each passing year. To my great disappointment, however, my father refused to disclose any further information about Uncle Petros beyond his dismissive incantation, 'one of life's failures'. From my mother I learned of his daily activities (one could hardly speak of an occupation): he got up every morning at the crack of dawn and spent most daylight hours slaving away in his garden, without help from a gardener or any modern labour-saving contraptions – his brothers erroneously attributed this to stinginess. He seldom left his house, except for a monthly visit to a small philanthropic institution founded by my grandfather, where he volunteered his services as treasurer. In addition, he sometimes went to 'another place', never specified by her. His house was a true hermitage; with the exception of the annual family invasion there were never any visitors. Uncle Petros had no social life of any kind. In the evenings he stayed at home and – here mother had lowered her voice almost to a whisper – 'immersed himself in his studies'.

At this my attention suddenly peaked. 'Studies? What studies?'

'God only knows,' answered Mother, conjuring up in my boyish imagination visions of esoterica, alchemy or worse.

A further unexpected piece of information came to identify the mysterious 'other place' that Uncle Petros visited. It was offered one evening by a dinner-guest of my father's.

'I saw your brother Petros at the club the other day. He demolished me with a Karo-Cann,' said the guest, and I interjected, earning an angry look from my father: 'What do you mean? What's a Karo-Cann?'

Our guest explained that he was referring to a particular way of opening the game of chess, named after its two inventors, Messrs Karo and Cann. Apparently, Uncle Petros was in the habit of paying occasional visits to a chess club in Patissia where he routinely routed his unfortunate opponents.

'What a player!' the guest sighed admiringly. 'If only he'd entered formal competition he'd be a Grand Master today!'

At this point Father changed the subject.

The annual family reunion was held in the garden. The grown-ups sat around a table that had been set up in a paved patio, drinking, snacking and making small-talk, the two younger brothers routinely exerting themselves (as a rule, not altogether successfully) to be gracious to the honouree. My cousins and I played among the trees in the orchard.

On one occasion, having made the decision to seek an answer to the mystery of Uncle Petros, I asked to use the bathroom; I was hoping I would get a chance to examine the inside of the house. To my great disappointment, however, our host indicated a small outhouse attached to the tool-shed. The next year (by that time I was fourteen) the weather came in aid of my curiosity. A summer storm forced my uncle to open the French windows and lead us into a space that had obviously been intended by the architect to serve as a living room. Equally obviously, however, the owner did not use it to receive guests. Although it did contain a couch, it was totally inappropriately positioned facing a blank wall. Chairs were brought in from the garden and placed in a semi-circle, where we sat like the mourners at a provincial wake.

I made a hasty reconnaissance, with quick glances all around. The only pieces of furniture apparently put to daily use were a deep, shabby armchair by the fireplace with a small table at its side; on it was a chessboard with the pieces set out as for a game in progress. Next to the table, on the floor, was a large pile of chess books and periodicals. This, then, was where Uncle

Petros sat every night. The studies mentioned by my mother must have been studies of chess. But were they?

I couldn't allow myself to jump to facile conclusions, as there were now new speculative possibilities. The main feature of the room we sat in – what made it so different from the living room in our house – was the overwhelming presence of books, countless books everywhere. Not only were all the visible walls of the room, corridor and entrance hall dressed from floor to ceiling with shelves crammed to overflowing, but books in tall piles covered most of the floor area as well. Most of them looked old and overused.

At first, I chose the most direct route to answering my question about their content: I asked, 'What are all these books, Uncle Petros?'

There was a frozen silence, exactly as if I had spoken of rope in the house of the hanged man.

'They are . . . old,' he mumbled hesitantly, after casting a quick glance in the direction of my father. He seemed so flustered in his search for an answer, however, and the accompanying smile was so wan that I couldn't bring myself to ask for further explanations.

Once again I resorted to the call of nature. This time Uncle Petros led me to a small toilet next to the kitchen. On my way back to the living room, alone and unobserved, I seized the opportunity I had created. I picked up the top book of the nearest pile in the corridor and flipped hurriedly through the pages. Unfortunately it was in German, a language I was (and still am) totally unfamiliar with. On top of it, most of the pages were adorned with mysterious symbols such as I'd never seen before: $\forall$'s and $\exists$'s and $\int$'s and $\notin$'s. Among them, I discerned some more intelligible signs, $+$'s, $=$'s and $\div$'s interspersed with numerals and letters both Latin and Greek. My rational mind overcame cabbalistic fantasies: it was mathematics!

I left Ekali that day totally preoccupied with my discovery, indifferent to the scolding I received from my father on the way back to Athens and to his hypocritical reprimands about my 'rudeness to my uncle' and 'my busybody, prying questions'. As if it was the breach in *savoir-vivre* that had bothered him!

My curiosity about Uncle Petros' dark, unknown side developed in the next few months into something approaching obsession. I remember compulsively drawing doodles combining mathematical and chess symbols in my notebooks during school classes. Maths and chess: in one of these most probably lay the solution to the mystery surrounding him, yet neither offered a totally satisfactory explanation, neither being reconcilable with his brothers' contemptuously dismissive attitude. Surely, these two fields of interest (or was it more than mere interest?) were not in themselves objectionable. Whichever way you looked at it, being a chess player at Grand Master level or a mathematician who had devoured hundreds of formidable tomes did not immediately classify you as 'one of life's failures'.

I needed to find out, and in order to do so I even contemplated for a while a venture in the style of the exploits of my favourite literary heroes, a project worthy of Enid Blyton's Secret Seven, the Hardy Boys, or their Greek soulmate, the 'heroic Phantom Boy'. I planned, down to the smallest detail, a break-in at my uncle's house during one of his expeditions to the philanthropic institution or the chess club, so I could lay my hands on palpable evidence of transgression.

As things turned out, I did not have to resort to crime to satisfy my curiosity. The answer I was seeking came and hit me, so to speak, over the head.

Here's how it happened:

One afternoon, while I was alone at home doing my homework, the phone rang and I answered it.

'Good evening,' said an unfamiliar male voice. 'I'm calling from the Hellenic Mathematical Society. May I speak to the Professor please?'

Unthinking at first, I corrected the caller: 'You must have dialled the wrong number. There is no professor here.'

'Oh, I'm sorry,' he said. 'I should have inquired first. Isn't that the Papachristos residence?'

I had a sudden flash of inspiration. 'Do you, perhaps, mean Mr *Petros* Papachristos?' I asked.

'Yes,' said the caller, '*Professor* Papachristos.'

'Professor'! The receiver nearly dropped from my hand. However, I suppressed my excitement, lest this windfall opportunity go to waste.

'Oh, I didn't realize you were referring to *Professor* Papachristos,' I said ingratiatingly. 'You see, this is his brother's home, but as the Professor does not have a telephone' – (fact) – 'we take his calls for him' (blatant lie).

'Could I then have his address?' the caller asked, but by now I had regained my composure and he was no match for me.

'The Professor likes to maintain his privacy,' I said haughtily. 'We also receive his mail.'

I had left the poor man no options. 'Then be so kind as to give me your address. On behalf of the Hellenic Mathematical Society, we would like to send him an invitation.'

The next few days I played sick so as to be at home at the usual time of mail delivery. I didn't have to wait long. On the third day after the phone-call I had the precious envelope in my hand. I waited till after midnight for my parents to go to sleep and then tiptoed to

the kitchen and steamed it open (another lesson culled
from boys' fiction).

I unfolded the letter and read:

Mr Petros Papachristos
f. Professor of Analysis
University of Munich

Honourable Professor,
    Our Society is planning a special session to commem-
orate Leonard Euler's two hundred and fiftieth birthday
with a lecture on 'Formal Logic and the Foundations of
Mathematics'.
    We would be greatly honoured, dear Professor, if you
would attend and address a short greeting to the
Society . . .

So: the man routinely dismissed by my dear father
as 'one of life's failures' was a Professor of Analysis at
the University of Munich – the significance of the little
'f.' preceding his unexpectedly prestigious title still
escaped me. As to the achievements of this Leonard
Euler, still remembered and honoured two hundred
and fifty years after his birth, I hadn't the slightest
clue.

The next Sunday morning I left home wearing my Boy
Scout uniform, but instead of going to the weekly
meeting I boarded the bus for Ekali, the letter from the

Hellenic Mathematical Society safely in my pocket. I found my uncle in an old hat and rolled-up sleeves, spade in hand, turning the soil in a vegetable plot. He was surprised to see me.

'What brings you here?' he asked.

I gave him the sealed envelope.

'You needn't have gone to the trouble,' he said, barely glancing at it. 'You could have put it in the mail.' Then he smiled kindly. 'Thank you anyway, Boy Scout. Does your father know you've come?'

'Uh, no,' I muttered.

'Then I better drive you home; your parents will be worried.'

I protested that it wasn't necessary, but he insisted. He climbed into his ancient, beat-up VW beetle, muddy boots and all, and we set out for Athens. On the way I attempted more than once to start a conversation on the subject of the invitation, but he switched to irrelevant matters like the weather, the correct season for tree-pruning and scouting.

He dropped me off at the corner nearest our house. 'Should I come upstairs and provide excuses?'

'No thanks, Uncle, that won't be necessary.'

However, it turned out that excuses were necessary. As my ill luck would have it, Father had called the club to ask me to pick something up on the way home and been informed of my absence. Naïvely, I blurted out the whole truth. As it turned out, this was the worst possible choice. If I'd lied and told him that I played truant from the meeting in order to indulge in forbidden cigarettes in the park, or even visit a house of ill-repute, he wouldn't have been quite so upset.

'Haven't I expressly forbidden you to have *anything* to do with that man?' he yelled at me, getting so red in the face that my mother started pleading with him to think of his blood pressure.

'No, Father,' I replied truthfully. 'As a matter of fact, you never have. Never!'

'But don't you *know* about him? Haven't I told you a *thousand times* about my brother Petros?'

'Oh, you've told me a thousand times that he's "one of life's failures", but so what? He's still your brother – my uncle. Was it so terrible to take the poor fellow his letter? And, come to think of it, I don't see how being "one of life's failures" applies to someone with the rank of Professor of Analysis at a great university!'

'The rank of *former* Professor of Analysis,' growled my father, settling the matter of the little 'f.'

Still fuming, he pronounced the sentence for what he termed my 'abominable act of inexcusable disobedience'. I could hardly believe the severity: for a month I would be confined to my room at all hours except those spent at school. Even my meals would have to be taken there and I would be allowed no spoken communication with himself, my mother, or anybody else!

I went to my room to begin my sentence, feeling a martyr for Truth.

Late that same night, my father knocked softly on my door and entered. I was at my desk reading and, obedient to his decree, didn't speak a word of greeting. He seated himself across from me on the bed and I knew from his expression something had changed. He now appeared calm, even slightly guilt-ridden. He began by announcing that the punishment he had meted out was 'perhaps a bit too harsh' and thus no longer applied, and subsequently asked my pardon for his manner – a piece of behaviour unprecedented and totally uncharacteristic of the man. He realized that his outburst had been unjust. It was unreasonable, he said – and of course I agreed with him – to expect me to understand something he had never taken the trouble to explain. He had never spoken openly to me about the matter of Uncle Petros and now the time had come for his 'grievous error' to be corrected. He wanted to tell me about his eldest brother. I, of course, was all ears.

This is what he told me:

Uncle Petros had, from early childhood, shown signs of exceptional ability in mathematics. In grade school he had impressed his teachers with his ease in arithmetic and in high school he had mastered abstractions in algebra, geometry and trigonometry with unbelievable facility. Words like 'prodigy' and even 'genius' were applied. Though a man of little formal education, their father, my grandfather, proved himself enlightened. Rather than divert Petros to more practical studies that would prepare him to work at his side in the family business, he had encouraged him to follow his heart. He had enrolled at a precocious age at the University of Berlin, from which he had graduated with honours at nineteen. He had earned his doctorate the next year and joined the faculty at the University of Munich as full professor at the amazing age of twenty-four – the youngest man ever to achieve this rank.

I listened, goggle-eyed. 'Hardly the progress of "one of life's failures",' I commented.

'I haven't finished yet,' warned my father.

At this point he digressed from his narrative. Without any prompting from me he spoke of himself and Uncle Anargyros and their feelings towards Petros. The two younger brothers had followed his successes with pride. Never for a moment did they feel the least bit envious – after all they too were doing extremely well at school, though in nowhere near as spectacular a manner as their genius of a brother. Still, they had never felt very close to him. Since early childhood, Petros had been a loner. Even when he'd still lived at home, Father and Uncle Anargyros hardly ever spent time with him; while they played with their friends he was in his room solving geometry problems. When he went abroad to university, Grandfather had them write polite letters to Petros ('Dear brother, We are well . . . etc.'), to which he would reply, infrequently, with a laconic acknowledgement on a postcard. In 1925, when the whole family travelled to Germany to visit him, he turned up at their few encounters behaving like a total stranger, absent-minded, anxious, obviously impatient to get back to whatever it was he was doing. After that they never saw him again until 1940 when Greece went to war with Germany and he had to return.

'Why?' I asked Father. 'To enlist?'

'Of course not! Your uncle never had patriotic – or any other, for that matter – feelings. It's just that once war was declared he was considered an enemy alien and had to leave Germany.'

'So why didn't he go elsewhere, to England or America, to some other great university? If he was such a great mathematician –'

My father interrupted me with an appreciative grunt, accompanied by a loud slap on his thigh.

'That's the point,' he snapped. 'That's the whole point: he was no longer a great mathematician!'

'What do you mean?' I asked. 'How can that be?'

There was a long, pregnant pause, a sign that the critical point in the narrative, the exact locus where the action changes direction from uphill to down, had been reached. My father leaned towards me, frowning ominously, and his next words came in a deep murmur, almost a groan:

'Your uncle, my son, committed the greatest of sins.'

'But what did he do, Father, tell me! Did he steal or rob or kill?'

'No, no, all these are simple misdemeanours compared to his crime! Mind you, it isn't I who deem it so but the Gospel, our Lord Himself: "Thou shalt not blaspheme against the Spirit!" Your Uncle Petros cast pearls before swine; he took something holy and sacred and great, and shamelessly defiled it!'

The unexpected theological twist put me for a moment on guard: 'And what exactly was that?'

'His *gift*, of course!' shouted my father. 'The great, unique gift that God had blessed him with, his phenomenal, unprecedented mathematical talent! The miserable fool wasted it; he squandered it and threw it out with the garbage. Can you imagine it? The ungrateful bastard never did one day's useful work in mathematics. Never! Nothing! Zero! '

'But *why*?' I asked.

'Oh, because his Illustrious Excellence was engaged with "Goldbach's Conjecture".'

'With *what*?'

Father made a distasteful grimace. 'Oh, a riddle of some sort, something of no interest to anyone except a handful of idlers playing intellectual games.'

'A riddle? You mean like a crossword puzzle?'

'No, a mathematical problem – but not just any problem: this "Goldbach's Conjecture" thing is considered to be one of the most difficult in the whole of mathematics. Can you imagine? The greatest minds on this planet had failed to solve it, but your smart aleck uncle decided at the age of twenty-one that he would be the one . . . Then, he proceeded to waste his life on it!'

I was rather confused by the course of his reasoning. 'Wait a minute, Father,' I said. 'Is *that* his crime? Pursuing the solution of the most difficult problem in the history of mathematics? Are you serious? Why, this is magnificent; it is absolutely fantastic!'

Father glared at me. 'Had he managed to solve it, it might be "magnificent" or "absolutely fantastic" or what have you – although it would still be totally useless, of course. But he *didn't*!'

He now got impatient with me, once again his usual self. 'Son, do you know the Secret of Life?' he asked with a scowl.

'No, I don't.'

Before divulging it to me he blew his nose with a

trumpeting sound into his monogrammed silk hand-
kerchief:

'The Secret of Life is always to set yourself attainable goals. They may be easy or difficult, depending
on the circumstances and your character and abilities,
but they should always be at-tai-na-ble! In fact, I think
I'll hang your Uncle Petros' portrait in your room,
with a caption: EXAMPLE TO BE AVOIDED!'

It's impossible as I write now, in middle age, to describe the turbulence caused in my adolescent heart
by this first, however prejudiced and incomplete,
account of Uncle Petros' story. My father had obviously intended it to serve as a cautionary tale and yet
for me his words had exactly the opposite effect:
instead of steering me away from his aberrant older
brother, they drew me towards him as to a brilliantly
shining star.

I was awestruck by what I'd learned. Exactly what
this famous 'Goldbach's Conjecture' was I didn't
know, nor at that time did I care very much to learn.
What fascinated me was that the kindly, withdrawn
and seemingly unassuming uncle of mine was in fact a
man who, by his own deliberate choice, had struggled
for years on end at the outermost boundaries of human
ambition. This man whom I'd known all my life, who
was in fact my close blood relative, had spent his whole

life striving to solve One of the Most Difficult Problems in the History of Mathematics! While his brothers were studying and getting married, raising children and running the family business, wearing out their lives along with the rest of nameless humanity in the daily routines of subsistence, procreation and killing time, he, Prometheus-like, had striven to cast light into the darkest and most inaccessible corner of knowledge.

The fact that he had finally failed in his endeavour not only did not lower him in my eyes but, on the contrary, raised him to the highest peak of excellence. Was this not, after all, the very definition of the plight of the Ideal Romantic Hero, to Fight the Great Battle Although You Know It To Be Desperate? In fact, was my uncle any different from Leonidas and his Spartan troops guarding Thermopylae? The last verses of Cavafy's poem I had learned at school seemed ideally applicable to him:

> ... But greatest honour befits them that foresee,
> As many do indeed foresee,
> That Ephialtes the Traitor will finally appear
> And thus the Persians will at last
> Go through the narrow straits.

Even before I'd heard Uncle Petros' story, his brothers' derogatory remarks, beyond exciting curiosity, had inspired my sympathy. (This, by the way, had been in contrast to my two cousins' reactions, who bought their fathers' contempt wholesale.) Now that I knew the truth – even this highly prejudiced version of it – I immediately elevated him to role model.

The first consequence of this was a change in my attitude towards mathematical subjects at school, which I had found till then rather boring, with a resultant dramatic improvement in my performance. When Father saw on the next report card that my grades in Algebra, Geometry and Trigonometry had shot up to honours level, he raised a perplexed eyebrow and gave me a queer look. It's possible that he even became slightly suspicious, but of course he couldn't make an issue of it. He could hardly criticize me for excelling!

On the date when the Hellenic Mathematical Society was due to commemorate Leonard Euler's two hundred and fiftieth birthday, I arrived ahead of time at the auditorium, full of expectation. Although high-school maths was of no help in fathoming its precise meaning, the announced lecture's title, 'Formal Logic and the Foundations of Mathematics', had intrigued me since first reading the invitation. I knew of 'formal receptions' and 'simple logic' but how did the two concepts combine? I'd learned that buildings have foundations – but mathematics?

I waited in vain, however, as the audience and the speakers took their places, to see among them the lean, ascetic figure of my uncle. As I should have guessed, he didn't come. I already knew he never accepted invitations; now I'd learned he didn't make exceptions even for mathematics.

The first speaker, the president of the Society, mentioned his name, and with particular respect:

'Professor Petros Papachristos, the world-renowned Greek mathematician, will unfortunately be unable to deliver his short address, because of a slight indisposition.'

I smiled smugly, proud that only I among the audience knew that my uncle's 'slight indisposition' was a diplomatic one, an excuse to protect his peace.

Despite Uncle Petros' absence, I stayed until the end of the event. I listened fascinated to a brief résumé of the honouree's life (Leonard Euler, apparently, had made epoch-making discoveries in practically every branch of mathematics). Then, as the main speaker took the podium and started elaborating on the 'Foundations of Mathematical Theories by Formal Logic', I fell into a charmed state. Despite the fact that I didn't completely understand more than the first few words of what he said, my spirit wallowed in the unfamiliar bliss of unknown definitions and concepts, all symbols of a world which, although mysterious, impressed me from the start as almost sacred in its unfathomable wisdom. Magical, previously unheard-of names rolled on and on, enthralling me with their sublime music: the Continuum Problem, Aleph, Tarski, Gottlob Frege, Inductive Reasoning, Hilbert's Programme, Proof Theory, Riemannian Geometry, Verifiability and Non-Verifiability, Consistency Proofs, Completeness Proofs, Sets of Sets, Universal Turing Machines, Von Neumann Automata, Russell's Paradox, Boolean Algebras.... At some point, in the midst of these intoxicating verbal waves washing over me, I thought for a moment I discerned the momentous words 'Goldbach's Conjecture'; but before I could focus my attention the subject had evolved along new magical pathways: Peano's Axioms for Arithmetic, the Prime Number Theorem, Closed and Open Systems, Axioms, Euclid, Euler, Cantor, Zeno, Gödel....

Paradoxically, the lecture on the 'Foundations of Mathematical Theories by Formal Logic' worked its insidious magic on my adolescent soul precisely because it disclosed none of the secrets that it introduced – I don't know whether it would have had the same effect had its mysteries been explained in detail. At last I understood the meaning of the sign at the entrance of Plato's Academy: *oudeis ageometretos eiseto* – 'Let no one ignorant of geometry enter'. The moral of my evening emerged with crystal clarity: mathematics was something infinitely more interesting than solving second-degree equations or calculating the volumes of solids, the menial tasks at which we laboured at school. Its practitioners dwelt in a veritable conceptual heaven, a majestic poetic realm totally inaccessible to the un-mathematical *hoi polloi*.

The evening at the Hellenic Mathematical Society was the turning point. It was then and there that I first resolved to become a mathematician.

At the end of that school year I was awarded the school prize for highest achievement in Mathematics. My father boasted about it to Uncle Anargyros – as if he could have done otherwise!

By now, I had completed my second-to-last year of high school and it had already been decided that I would be attending university in the United States. As the American system doesn't require students to declare their major field of interest upon registration, I could defer revealing to my father the horrible (as he would no doubt consider it) truth for a few more years. (Luckily, my two cousins had already stated a preference that assured the family business of a new generation of managers.) In fact, I misled him for a while with vague talk of plans to study economics, while I was hatching my plan: once I was safely enrolled in university, with the whole Atlantic Ocean between me and his authority, I could steer my course toward my destiny.

That year, on the feast day of Saints Peter and Paul, I

couldn't hold back any longer. At some point I drew Uncle Petros aside and, impulsively, I blurted my intention.

'Uncle, I'm thinking of becoming a mathematician.'

My enthusiasm, however, found no immediate response. My uncle remained silent and impassive, his gaze suddenly focused on my face with intense seriousness – with a shiver I realized that this was what he must have looked like as he was struggling to penetrate the mysteries of Goldbach's Conjecture.

'What do you know of mathematics, young man?' he asked after a short pause.

I didn't like his tone but I went on as planned: 'I was first in my class, Uncle Petros; I received the school prize!'

He seemed to consider this information awhile and then shrugged. 'It's an important decision,' he said, 'not to be taken without serious deliberation. Why don't you come here one afternoon and we'll talk about it.' Then he added, unnecessarily: 'It's better if you don't tell your father.'

I went a few days later, as soon as I could arrange a good cover story.

Uncle Petros led me to the kitchen and offered me a cold drink made from the sour cherries from his tree. Then he took a seat across from me, looking solemn and professorial.

'So tell me,' he asked, 'what is mathematics in your *opinion*?' The emphasis on the last word seemed to carry the implication that whatever answer I gave was bound to be wrong.

I spurted out commonplaces about 'the most supreme of sciences' and the wonderful applications in electronics, medicine and space exploration.

Uncle Petros frowned. 'If you're interested in applications why don't you become an engineer? Or a physicist. They too are involved with some *sort* of mathematics.'

Another emphasis with meaning: obviously he didn't hold this 'sort' in very high esteem. Before I embarrassed myself further, I decided that I was not equipped to spar with him as an equal, and confessed it.

'Uncle, I can't put the "why" into words. All I know is that I want to be a mathematician – I thought you'd understand.'

He considered this for a while and then asked: 'Do you know chess?'

'Sort of, but please don't ask me to play; I can tell you right now I'm going to lose!'

He smiled. 'I wasn't suggesting a game; I just want to give you an example that you'll understand. Look, real mathematics has nothing to do with applications, nor with the calculating procedures that you learn at school. It studies abstract intellectual constructs which, at least while the mathematician is occupied with them, do not in any way touch on the physical, sensible world.'

'That's all right with me,' I said.

'Mathematicians,' he continued, 'find the same enjoyment in their studies that chess players find in chess. In fact, the psychological make-up of the true mathematician is closer to that of the poet or the musical composer, in other words of someone concerned with the creation of Beauty and the search for Harmony and Perfection. He is the polar opposite of the practical man, the engineer, the politician or the . . .' – he paused for a moment seeking something even more abhorred in his scale of values – '. . . indeed, the businessman.'

If he was telling me all this in order to discourage me, he had chosen the wrong route.

'That's what I'm after too, Uncle Petros,' I responded excitedly. 'I don't want to be an engineer; I don't want to work in the family business. I want to immerse myself in *real* mathematics, just like you . . . just like Goldbach's Conjecture!'

I'd blown it! Before I'd left for Ekali I had decided that any reference to the Conjecture should be avoided like the devil during our conversation. But in my carelessness and excitement I'd let it slip out.

Although Uncle Petros remained expressionless, I noticed a slight tremor run down his hand. 'Who's spoken to you about Goldbach's Conjecture?' he asked quietly.

'My father,' I murmured.

'And what did he say, precisely?'

'That you tried to prove it.'

'Just that?'

'And . . . and that you didn't succeed.'

His hand was steady again. 'Nothing else?'

'Nothing else.'

'Hm,' he said. 'Suppose we make a deal?'

'What sort of a deal?'

'Listen to me: the way I see things, in mathematics as in the arts – or in sports, for that matter – if you're not the best, you're nothing. A civil engineer, or a lawyer, or a dentist who is merely capable may yet lead a creative and fulfilling professional life. However, a mathematician who is just average – I'm talking about a researcher, of course, not a high-school teacher – is a living, walking tragedy . . .'

'But Uncle,' I interrupted, 'I haven't the slightest intention of being "just average". I want to be Number One!'

He smiled. 'In that at least you definitely resemble me. I too was overambitious. But you see, dear boy, good intentions are, alas, not enough. This is not like many other fields where diligence always pays. To get to the top in mathematics you also need something more, the absolutely necessary condition for success.'

'Which one is that?'

He gave me a puzzled look, for ignoring the obvious.

'Why, the talent! The natural predisposition in its more extreme manifestation. Never forget it: *Mathematicus nascitur, non fit* – A mathematician is born, not made. If you don't carry the special aptitude in your genes, you will labour in vain all your life and one day you will end up a mediocrity. A golden mediocrity, perhaps, but a mediocrity nevertheless!'

I looked him straight in the eye.

'What's your deal, Uncle?'

He hesitated for a moment, as if thinking it over. Then he said: 'I don't want to see you following a course that will lead to failure and unhappiness. Therefore I'm proposing that you will make a binding promise to me to become a mathematician if and only if you're supremely gifted. Do you accept?'

I was disconcerted. 'But how on earth can I determine that, Uncle?'

'You can't and you don't need to,' he said with a sly little smile. '*I* will.'

'You?'

'Yes. I will set you a problem, which you will take

home with you and attempt to solve. By your success, or failure, I will measure your potential for mathematical greatness with great accuracy.'

I had mixed feelings for the proposed deal: I hated tests but adored challenges.

'How much time will I have?' I asked.

Uncle Petros half-closed his eyes, considering this. 'Mmm . . . Let's say till the beginning of school, the first of October. That gives you almost three months.'

Ignorant as I was, I believed that in three months I could solve not one but any number of mathematical problems.

'*That* much!'

'Well, the problem will be difficult,' he pointed out. 'It's not one just anybody can solve, but if you've got what it takes to become a great mathematician, you will manage. Of course, you will swear that you will seek help from no one and you will not consult any books.'

'I swear,' I said.

He fixed his stare on me. 'Does that mean you accept the deal?'

I heaved a deep sigh. 'I do!'

Without a word, Uncle Petros disappeared briefly and returned with paper and pencil. He now became businesslike, mathematician to mathematician.

'Here's the problem . . . I assume you already know what a prime number is?'

'Of course I know, Uncle! A prime is an integer greater than 1 that has no divisors other than itself and unity. For example 2, 3, 5, 7, 11, 13, and so on.'

He appeared pleased with the precision of my definition. 'Wonderful! Now tell me, please, how many prime numbers are there?'

I suddenly felt out of my depth. 'How *many*?'

'Yes, how *many*. Haven't they taught you that at school?'

'No.'

My uncle sighed a deep sigh of disappointment at the low quality of modern Greek mathematical education.

'All right, I will tell you this because you will need it: the primes are infinite, a fact first proven by Euclid in the third century BC. His proof is a gem of beauty and simplicity. By using *reductio ad absurdum*, he first assumes the contrary of what he wants to prove, namely that the primes are finite. So . . .'

With fast vigorous jabs at the paper and a few explanatory words Uncle Petros laid out for my benefit our wise ancestor's proof, also giving me my first example of real mathematics.

'. . . which, however,' he concluded, 'is contrary to our initial assumption. Assuming finiteness leads to a contradiction; *ergo* the primes are infinite. *Quod erat demonstrandum.*'

'That's fantastic, Uncle,' I said, exhilarated by the ingeniousness of the proof. 'It's so simple!'

'Yes,' he sighed, 'so simple, yet no one had thought of it before Euclid. Consider the lesson behind this: sometimes things appear simple only in retrospect.'

I was in no mood for philosophizing. 'Go on now, Uncle. State the problem I have to solve!'

First he wrote it out on a piece of paper and then he read it to me.

'I want you to try to demonstrate,' he said, 'that every even number greater than 2 is the sum of two primes.'

I considered it for a moment, fervently praying for a flash of inspiration that would blow him away with an instant solution. As it wasn't forthcoming, however, I just said: 'That's all?'

Uncle Petros wagged his finger in warning. 'Ah, it's not that simple! For every particular case you can consider, $4 = 2 + 2, 6 = 3 + 3, 8 = 3 + 5, 10 = 3 + 7, 12 = 7 + 5, 14 = 7 + 7$, etc., it's obvious, although the bigger the numbers get the more extensive the calculating. However, since there is an infinity of evens, a case-by-case approach is not possible. You have to find a general demonstration and this, I suspect, you may find more difficult than you think.'

I got up. 'Difficult or not,' I said, 'I will do it! I'm going to start work right away.'

As I was on my way to the gate he called from the kitchen window. 'Hey! Aren't you going to take the paper with the problem?'

A cold wind was blowing and I breathed in the exhalation of the moist soil. I don't think that ever in my life, whether before or after that brief moment, have I felt so happy, so full of promise and anticipation and glorious hope.

'I don't need to, Uncle,' I called back. 'I remember it perfectly: Every even number greater than 2 is the sum of two primes. See you on October the first with the solution!'

His stern reminder found me in the street: 'Don't forget our deal,' he shouted. 'Only if you solve the problem can you become a mathematician!'

A rough summer lay in store for me.

Luckily, my parents always packed me off to my maternal uncle's house in Pylos for the hot months, July and August. That meant that, removed from my father's range, at least I didn't have the additional problem (as if the one Uncle Petros had set me were not enough) of having to conduct my work in secret. As soon as I arrived in Pylos I spread out my papers on the dining-room table (we always ate outdoors in the summer) and declared to my cousins that until further notice I would not be available for swimming, games and visits to the open-air movie theatre. I began to work at the problem from morning to night, with minimal interruption.

My aunt fussed in her good-natured manner: 'You're working too much, dear boy. Take it easy. It's summer vacation. Leave the books aside for a while. You came here to rest.'

I, however, was determined not to rest until final victory. I slaved at my table incessantly, scribbling away on sheet after sheet of paper, approaching the problem from this side and that. Often, when I felt too exhausted for abstract deductive reasoning, I would test specific cases, lest Uncle Petros had set me a trap by asking me to demonstrate something obviously false. After countless divisions I had created a table of the first few hundred primes (a primitive, self-made Eratosthenes' Sieve*) which I then proceeded to add, in all possible pairs, to confirm that the principle indeed applied. In vain did I search for an even number within this boundary that didn't fit the required condition – all of them turned out to be expressible as the sum of two primes.

At some point in mid-August, after a succession of late nights and countless Greek coffees, I thought for a few happy hours that I'd got it, that I'd found

---

* A method for locating the primes, invented by the Greek mathematician Eratosthenes.

the solution. I filled several pages with my reasoning and mailed them, by special delivery, to Uncle Petros.

I had barely enjoyed my triumph for a few days when the postman brought me the telegram:

THE ONLY THING YOU HAVE DEMONSTRATED IS
THAT EVERY EVEN NUMBER CAN BE EXPRESSED AS
THE SUM OF ONE PRIME AND ONE ODD WHICH
HOWEVER IS OBVIOUS STOP

It took me a week to recover from the failure of my first attempt and the blow to my pride. But recover I did and half-heartedly I resumed work, this time employing the *reductio ad absurdum*:

'Let us assume there is an even number n which *cannot* be expressed as the sum of two primes. Then...'

The longer I laboured on the problem the more apparent it became that it expressed a fundamental truth regarding the integers, the *materia prima* of the mathematical universe. Soon I was driven to wondering about the precise way in which the primes are distributed among the other integers or the procedure which, given a certain prime, leads us to the next. I knew that this information, were I to possess it, would be extremely useful in my plight and once or twice I was tempted to search for it in a book. However, loyal to my commitment not to seek outside help, I never did.

By stating Euclid's demonstration of the infinity of the primes, Uncle Petros said he'd given me the only tool I needed to find the proof. Yet I was making no progress.

At the end of September, a few days before the beginning of my last year in school, I found myself once again in Ekali, morose and crestfallen. Since Uncle Petros didn't have a telephone, I had to go through with this in person.

'Well?' he asked me as soon as we sat down, after I'd stiffly refused his offer of a sour-cherry drink. 'Did you solve the problem?'

'No,' I said. 'As a matter of fact, I didn't.'

The last thing I wanted at that point was to have to trace the course of my failure or have him analyse it for my sake. What's more, I had absolutely no curiosity to learn the solution, the proof of the principle. All I wished was to forget everything even remotely related to numbers, whether odd or even – not to mention prime.

But Uncle Petros wasn't willing to let me off easily. 'That's that then,' he said. 'You remember our deal, don't you?'

I found his need officially to ratify his victory (as, for some reason, I was certain he viewed my defeat) intensely annoying. Yet I wasn't planning to make it sweeter for him by displaying any hint of hurt feelings.

'Of course I do, Uncle, as I'm sure you do too. Our deal was that I wouldn't become a mathematician unless I solved the problem –'

'No!' he cut me off, with sudden vehemence. 'The deal was that unless you solved the problem you'd *make a binding promise* not to become a mathematician!'

I scowled at him. 'Precisely,' I agreed. 'And as I haven't solved the problem –'

'You will now *make a binding promise*,' he interrupted, a second time completing the sentence, stressing the words as if his life (or mine, rather) depended on it.

'Sure,' I said, forcing myself to sound nonchalant, 'if it pleases you, I'll make a binding promise.'

His voice became harsh, cruel even. 'It's not a question of *pleasing* me, young man, but of honouring our agreement! You will pledge to stay away from mathematics!'

My annoyance instantly developed into full-fledged hatred.

'All right, Uncle,' I said coldly. 'I pledge to stay away from mathematics. Happy now?'

But as I got up to go he lifted his hand, menacingly. 'Not so fast!'

With a quick move he got a sheet of paper out of his pocket, unfolded it and stuck it in front of my nose. This was it:

I, the undersigned, being in full possession of my faculties, hereby solemnly pledge that, having failed in my examination for a higher mathematical capability and in accordance with the agreement made with my uncle, Petros Papachristos, I will never work towards a mathematics degree at an institution of higher learning, nor in any other way attempt to pursue a professional career in mathematics.

I stared at him in disbelief.

'Sign!' he commanded.

'What's the use of this?' I growled, now making no effort to conceal my feelings.

'Sign,' he repeated unmoved. 'A deal is a deal!'

I left his extended hand holding the fountain pen suspended in mid-air, got out my ballpoint and jabbed in my signature. Before he had time to say anything more I threw the paper at him and made a wild rush to the gate.

'Wait!' he shouted, but I was already outside.

I ran and ran and ran until I was safely out of his hearing and then I stopped and, still breathless, broke down and cried like a baby, tears of anger and frustration and humiliation streaming down my face.

I neither saw nor spoke to Uncle Petros during my last year of school, and in the following June I made up an excuse to my father and stayed home during the traditional family visit to Ekali.

My experience of the previous summer had had the exact result that Uncle Petros had, doubtless, intended and foreseen. Irrespective of any obligation to keep my part of our 'deal', I had lost all desire to become a mathematician. Luckily, the side effects of my failure were not extreme, my rejection was not total and my superior performance at school continued. As a consequence, I was admitted to one of the best universities in the United States. Upon registration I declared a major in Economics, a choice I abided by till my Junior year.* Apart from the basic requirements, Elementary Calculus and Linear Algebra (incidentally, I got As in both), I took no other mathematics courses in my first two years.

Uncle Petros' successful (at first, anyway) ploy had been based on the application of the absolute determinism of mathematics to my life. He had taken a risk, of course, but it was a well-calculated one: the

---

* According to the American system, a student can go through the first two years of university without being obliged to declare an area of major concentration for his degree or, if he does so, is free to change his mind until the beginning of the Junior (third) year.

possibility of my discovering the identity of the problem he had assigned me in the course of elementary university mathematics was minimal. The field to which it belongs is Number Theory, only taught in electives aimed at mathematics majors. Therefore it was reasonable for him to assume that, as long as I kept my pledge, I would complete my university studies (and conceivably my life) without learning the truth.

Reality, however, is not as dependable as mathematics, and things turned out differently.

On the first day of my Junior year I was informed that Fate (for who else can arrange coincidences such as this?) had assigned that I share my dormitory room with Sammy Epstein, a slightly built boy from Brooklyn renowned among undergraduates as a phenomenal maths prodigy. Sammy would be getting his degree that same year at the age of seventeen and, although he was nominally still an undergraduate, all his classes were already at advanced graduate level. In fact, he had already started work on his doctoral dissertation in Algebraic Topology.

Convinced as I was until that point that the wounds of my short traumatic history as a mathematics hopeful had more or less healed, I was delighted, even amused, when I learned the identity of my new room-mate. As we were dining side by side in the university dining hall on our first evening, to get better acquainted, I said to him casually:

'Since you're a mathematical genius, Sammy, I'm sure you can easily prove that every even number greater than 2 is the sum of two primes.'

He burst out laughing. 'If I could prove *that*, man, I wouldn't be here eating with you; I'd be a professor already. Maybe I'd even have my Fields Medal, the Nobel Prize of Mathematics!'

Even as he was speaking, in a flash of revelation, I guessed the awful truth. Sammy confirmed it with his next words:

'The statement you just made is Goldbach's Conjecture, one of the most notoriously difficult unsolved problems in the whole of mathematics!'

My reactions went through the phases referred to (if I accurately remember what I learned in my elementary college Psychology course) as the Four Stages of Mourning: Denial, Anger, Depression and Acceptance.

Of these, the first was the most short-lived. 'It . . . it can't be!' I stammered as soon as Sammy had uttered the horrible words, hoping I'd misheard.

'What do you mean "it can't be"?' he asked. 'It can and it is! Goldbach's Conjecture – that's the name of the hypothesis, for it is only a hypothesis, since it's never been proved – is that all evens are the sum of two primes. It was first stated by a mathematician named Goldbach in a letter to Euler.* Although it's been tested and found to be true up to enormous even numbers, no one has managed to find a general proof.'

I didn't hear Sammy's next words, for I had already passed into the stage of Anger:

'The old bastard!' I yelled in Greek. 'The son of a bitch! God damn him! May he rot in hell!'

My new room-mate, totally bewildered that a hypothesis in Number Theory could provoke such an outburst of violent Mediterranean passion, pleaded with me to tell him what was going on. I, however, was in no state for explanations.

I was nineteen and until then had led a protected life. Except for the single Scotch drunk with Father to celebrate, 'among grown-up men', my graduation from high school and the required sip of wine to toast a relative's wedding, I had never tasted alcohol. Consequently, the great quantities I put down that night at a bar near the university (I started out with beer, moved

---

* In fact, Christian Goldbach's letter of 1742 contains the conjecture that 'every integer can be expressed as the sum of three primes'. However, as (if this is true) one of the three such primes expressing even numbers will be 2 (the addition of three odd primes would be of necessity odd, and 2 is the only even prime number), it is an obvious corollary that every even number is the sum of two primes. Ironically, it was not Goldbach but Euler who phrased the conjecture that bears the other's name – a little known fact, even among mathematicians.

on to bourbon and ended up with rum) must be multiplied by a rather large n to fully realize their effect.

While on my third or fourth glass of beer and still in moderate possession of my senses, I wrote to Uncle Petros. Later, once into the phase of fatalistic certainty as to my imminent death, and before I passed out, I handed over the letter to the barman with his address and what remained of my monthly allowance, asking him to fulfil my last wish and mail it. The partial amnesia that cloaks the events of that night has obscured for ever the detailed content of the letter. (I did not have the emotional stamina to seek it out from among my uncle's papers, when many years later I inherited his archive.) From the little that I remember, however, there can be no swear-word, vulgarity, insult, condemnation and curse that it didn't contain. The gist of it was that he had destroyed my life and as a consequence upon my return to Greece I would murder him, but this only after torturing him in the most perverse ways human imagination could contrive.

I don't know how long I remained unconscious, struggling with outlandish nightmares. It must have been late afternoon of the following day before I began to be aware of my surroundings. I was in my bed in the dormitory and Sammy was there, at his desk, bent over his books. I groaned. He came over and explained:

-45-

I had been brought back by some fellow students who'd found me dead to the world on the lawn in front of the library. They'd hauled me to the infirmary, where the doctor on duty had had no difficulty diagnosing my condition. As a matter of fact, he didn't even have to examine me, as my clothes were covered in vomit and I reeked of alcohol.

My new room-mate, obviously concerned about the future of our cohabitation, asked me whether this sort of thing occurred frequently with me. Humiliated, I mumbled that it was the first time.

'It's all because of Goldbach's Conjecture,' I whispered, and sank back into sleep.

It took me two days to recover from an excruciating headache. After that (it seems the torrent of alcohol had carried me right through Rage) I entered the next stage of my mourning: Depression. For two days and nights I stayed slumped in an armchair in the common room on our floor, listlessly observing the black-and-white images dancing on the TV screen.

It was Sammy who helped me out of this self-inflicted lethargy, displaying a sense of camaraderie totally inconsistent with the caricature of the self-centred, absent-minded mathematician. On the evening of the third day after my bender I saw him standing there, looking down at me.

'Do you know tomorrow is the deadline for registration?' he asked severely.

'Mmmm . . .' I groaned.

'So, have you registered?'

I shook my head wearily.

'Have you at least selected the courses you'll be taking?'

I shook my head once again and he frowned.

'Not that it's any of my business, but don't you think you better turn your attention to these rather urgent matters, instead of sitting there all day staring at the idiot-box?'

As he later confessed, it wasn't merely the urge to assist a fellow human being in crisis that made him assume responsibility – the curiosity to discover the connection between his new room-mate and the notorious mathematical problem was overwhelming. One thing is certain: regardless of his motives, the long discussion I had that evening with Sammy made all the difference to me. Without his understanding and support, I couldn't have crossed the crucial line. And, what's perhaps more important: it's quite unlikely I would ever have forgiven Uncle Petros.

We started our talk in the dining hall, over dinner, and continued through the night in our room, drinking coffee. I told him everything: about my family, my early fascination with the remote figure of Uncle Petros and my gradual discoveries of his accomplishments, his brilliant chess-playing, his books, the invitation of the Hellenic Mathematical Society and the professorship in Munich. About Father's brief résumé of his life, his early successes and the mysterious (to me, at least) role of Goldbach's Conjecture in his later dismal failure. I mentioned my initial decision to study mathematics and the discussion with Uncle Petros that summer afternoon, three years back, in his kitchen in Ekali. Finally, I described our 'deal'.

Sammy listened without interrupting once, his small, deep eyes narrowed intently in focus. Only when I reached the end of my narrative and stated the problem that my uncle had required me to solve to demonstrate my potential for mathematical greatness did he burst out, seized by sudden fury.

'What an ass-hole!' he cried.

'My feelings exactly,' I said.

'The man is a sadist,' Sammy went on. 'Why, he's criminally insane! Only a perverted mind could conceive the plot of making a school-kid spend a summer trying to solve Goldbach's Conjecture, and this under the illusion that he had merely been set a challenging exercise. What a total beast!'

The guilt about the extreme vocabulary I had used in my delirious letter to Uncle Petros led me for a moment to attempt to defend him and find a logical excuse for his behaviour.

'Maybe his intentions were not all bad,' I muttered. 'Maybe he thought he was protecting me from greater disappointment.'

'With what *right*?' Sammy said loudly, banging his hand on my desk. (Unlike me, he'd grown up in a society where children were not expected as a rule to conform to the expectations of their parents and elders.) 'Every person has the right to expose himself to whatever disappointment he chooses,' he said fervently. 'Besides, what's all this crap about "being the best" and "golden mediocrities" and whatnot. You could have become a great –'

Sammy stopped in mid-sentence, his mouth gaping in amazement. 'Wait a minute, why am I using the past tense?' he said, beaming. 'You can *still become* a great mathematician!'

I glanced up, startled. 'What are you talking about, Sammy? It's too late, you know that!'

'Not at all! The deadline for declaring a major is tomorrow.'

'That's not what I mean. I've already lost so much time doing other things and –'

'Nonsense,' he said firmly. 'If you work hard you can make up for lost time. What's important is that you recover your enthusiasm, the passion you had for mathematics before your uncle shamelessly destroyed it for you. Believe me, it can be done – and I'll help you do it!'

Day was breaking outside and the moment had come for the fourth and last stage that would complete the mourning process: Acceptance. The cycle had closed. I would pick up my life from where I'd left off when Uncle Petros, through the appalling trick he'd played on me, steered me away from what I then still considered my true course.

Sammy and I consumed a hearty breakfast in the dining hall and then sat down with the list of courses offered by the Department of Mathematics. He explained the contents of each one the way an experienced maître d' might present choice items on the menu. I took notes, and in the early afternoon I went to the Registrar's office and filed my selection of courses for the semester just beginning: Introduction to Analysis, Introduction to Complex Analysis, Introduction to Modern Algebra and General Topology.

Naturally, I also declared my new field of major concentration: Mathematics.

A few days after the beginning of classes, during the most difficult phase of my efforts to penetrate into the new discipline, a telegram from Uncle Petros arrived. When I found the notice, I had no doubts as to the identity of the sender and initially considered not claiming it at all. However, curiosity finally prevailed.

I made a bet with myself as to whether he would be trying to defend himself, or simply scolding me for the tone of my letter. I opted for the latter and lost. He wrote:

I FULLY UNDERSTAND YOUR REACTION STOP IN ORDER TO UNDERSTAND MY BEHAVIOUR YOU SHOULD ACQUAINT YOURSELF WITH KURT GÖDEL'S INCOMPLETENESS THEOREM

At that time I had no idea what Kurt Gödel's Incompleteness Theorem was. Also, I had no desire to find out – mastering the theorems of Lagrange, Cauchy, Fatou, Bolzano, Weierstrass, Heine, Borel, Lebesgue, Tychonoff, et al. for my various courses was hard enough. Anyway, by now I had more or less come to accept Sammy's assessment that Uncle Petros' behaviour towards me showed definite signs of derangement. The latest message confirmed this: he was trying to defend his despicable treatment of me by way of a mathematical theorem! The wretched old man's obsessions were of no further interest to me.

I did not mention the telegram to my room-mate, nor did I give it further thought.

*

I spent that Christmas vacation studying with Sammy at the Mathematics Library.*

On New Year's Eve he invited me to celebrate with him and his family at their Brooklyn home. We'd been drinking and were feeling quite merry when he took me aside to a quiet corner.

'Could you bear to talk about your uncle a bit?' he asked. Since that first, all-night session, the subject had never again come up, as if by unspoken agreement.

'Sure I can bear it,' I laughed, 'but what more is there to say?'

Sammy took out of his pocket a sheet of paper and unfolded it. 'It's been a while now since I've been doing some discreet research on the subject,' he said.

I was surprised. 'What kind of "discreet research"?'

'Oh, don't go imagining anything nefarious; mostly bibliographical stuff.'

'And?'

'And I came to the conclusion that your dear Uncle Petros is a fraud!'

'A *fraud*?' It was the last thing I would have expected to hear about him and, since blood is thicker

* The main purpose of this narrative is not autobiographical, so I will not burden the reader further with details of my own mathematical progress. (To satisfy the curious I could sum it up as 'slow but steady'.) Henceforth, my own story will be referred to only to the extent to which it is relevant to that of Uncle Petros.

than water, I immediately jumped to his defence.

'How can you say that, Sammy? It's a proven fact that he was Professor of Analysis at the University of Munich. He is no fraud!'

He explained: 'I went through the bibliographical indexes of all articles published in mathematical journals in this century. I only found three items under his name, but nothing – not *one single word* – on the subject of Goldbach's Conjecture or anything remotely related to it!'

I couldn't understand how this led to accusations of fraud. 'What's so surprising in that? My uncle is the first to admit that he didn't manage to prove the Conjecture: there was nothing to publish. I find it perfectly understandable!'

Sammy smiled condescendingly.

'That's because you don't know the first thing about research,' he said. 'Do you know what the great David Hilbert answered when questioned by his colleagues as to why he never attempted to prove the so-called "Fermat's Last Theorem", another famous unsolved problem?'

'No, I don't. Enlighten me.'

'He said: "Why should I kill the goose that lays the golden eggs?" What he meant, you see, was that when great mathematicians attempt to solve great problems a lot of great mathematics – so-called "intermediate results" – is born, and this even though the initial problems may remain unsolved. Just to give you an example you'll understand, the field of Finite Group Theory came into being as a result of Evariste Galois' efforts to solve the equation of the fifth degree in its general form . . .'

The gist of Sammy's argument was this: there was no way that a top-class professional mathematician, as we had every indication that Uncle Petros was in his youth, could have spent his life wrestling with a great problem such as Goldbach's Conjecture without discovering along the way a *single* intermediate result of some value. However, since he had never published anything, we necessarily had to conclude (here Sammy was applying a form of the *reductio ad absurdum*) that he was lying: he never had attempted to prove Goldbach's Conjecture.

'But to what purpose would he tell such a lie?' I asked my friend, perplexed.

'Oh, it's more likely than not that he concocted the Goldbach Conjecture story to explain his mathematical inactivity – this is why I used the harsh word "fraud". You see, this is a problem so notoriously difficult that nobody could hold it against him if he didn't manage to solve it.'

'But this is absurd,' I protested. 'Mathematics was Uncle Petros' life, his only interest and passion! Why would he want to abandon it and need to make up excuses for his inactivity? It doesn't make sense!'

Sam shook his head. 'The explanation, I'm afraid, is rather depressing. A distinguished professor in our department, with whom I discussed the case, suggested it to me.' He must have seen the signs of dismay in my face, for he hastened to add: '. . . without mentioning your uncle's name, of course!'

Sammy then outlined the 'distinguished professor's' theory: 'It's quite likely that at some point early in his career your uncle lost either the intellectual capacity or the willpower (or possibly both) to do mathematics. Unfortunately, this is quite common with early developers. Burnout and breakdown are the fate of quite a few precocious geniuses . . .'

The distressing possibility that this sorry fate could possibly also one day await himself had obviously entered his mind: the conclusion was spoken solemnly, sadly even.

'You see, it's not that your poor Uncle Petros didn't want after a certain point to do any more mathematics – it's that he *couldn't*.'

After my talk with Sammy on New Year's Eve, my attitude towards Uncle Petros changed once again. The rage I had felt when I first realized he had tricked me into attempting to prove Goldbach's Conjecture had already given way to more charitable feelings. Now, an element of sympathy was added: how terrible it must have been for him, if after such a brilliant beginning he suddenly began to feel his great gift, his only strength in life, his only joy, deserting him. Poor Uncle Petros!

The more I thought about it, the more I became upset at the unnamed 'distinguished professor' who could pronounce such damning indictments of someone he didn't even know, in the total absence of data. At Sammy, too. How could he so lightheartedly accuse him of being a 'fraud'?

I ended up deciding that Uncle Petros should be given the chance to defend himself, and to counter both the facile levelling generalizations of his brothers ('one of life's failures', etc.) as well as the condescending analyses of the 'distinguished professor' and the cocky boy-genius Sammy. The time had come for the accused to speak. Needless to say, I decided the person best qualified to hear his defence was none other than I, his close kin and victim. After all, he owed me.

I needed to prepare myself.

Although I had torn his telegram of apology into little pieces, I hadn't forgotten its content. My uncle had enjoined me to learn Kurt Gödel's Incompleteness Theorem; in some unfathomable way the explanation of his despicable behaviour to me lay in this. (Without knowing the first thing about the Incompleteness Theorem I didn't like the sound of it: the negative particle 'in-' carried a lot of baggage; the vacuum it hinted at seemed to have metaphorical implications.)

At the first opportunity, which came while selecting my mathematics courses for the next semester, I asked Sammy, careful not to have him suspect that my question had anything to do with Uncle Petros: 'Have you ever heard of Kurt Gödel's Incompleteness Theorem?'

Sammy threw his arms in the air, in comic exaggeration. 'Oy vey!' he exclaimed. 'He asks me if I've heard of Kurt Gödel's Incompleteness Theorem!'

'To what branch does it belong? Topology?'

Sammy stared at me aghast. 'The *Incompleteness* Theorem? – to Mathematical Logic, you total ignoramus!'

'Well, stop clowning and tell me about it. Tell me what it says.'

Sammy proceeded to explain along general lines the content of Gödel's great discovery. He began from Euclid and his vision of the solid construction of mathematical theories, starting from axioms as foundations and proceeding by the tools of rigorous logical induction to theorems. Then, he spanned twenty-two centuries to talk of 'Hilbert's Second Problem' and skimmed over the basics of Russell's and Whitehead's *Principia Mathematica*,* terminating

---

* *Principia Mathematica*: the monumental work of logicians Russell and Whitehead, first published in 1910, in which they attempt the titanic task of founding the edifice of mathematical theories on the firm foundations of logic.

with the Incompleteness Theorem itself, which he explained in as simple language as he could.

'But is that possible?' I asked when he was finished, staring at him wide-eyed.

'More than possible,' answered Sammy, 'it's a proven *fact*!'

Two

I went to Ekali on the second day after my arrival in Greece for the summer vacation. Not wanting to catch him unawares, I'd already arranged the meeting with Uncle Petros by correspondence. To continue with the judicial analogy, I'd granted him ample time to prepare his defence.

I arrived at the arranged time and we sat in the garden.

'So then, most favoured of nephews' (this was the first time he called me that), 'what news do you bring me from the New World?'

If he thought I'd let him pretend this was a mere social occasion, a visit by dutiful nephew to caring uncle, he was mistaken.

'So then, Uncle,' I said belligerently, 'in a year's time I'm getting my degree and I'm already preparing applications for graduate school. Your ploy has failed. Whether it is to your liking or not, I will be a mathematician.'

He shrugged his shoulders while raising the palms of his hands heavenwards in a gesture of inevitability.

'"He who is fated to drown will never die in his bed",' he intoned – a popular Greek proverb. 'Have you told your father? Is he pleased?'

'Why this sudden interest in my father?' I snarled. 'Was it he who put you up to our so-called "deal"? Was it his perverse idea to make me prove myself worthy by tackling Goldbach's Conjecture? Or do you feel so much in his debt for supporting you all these years that you repaid him by bringing his upstart son to heel?'

Uncle Petros accepted the blows under the belt without changing expression.

'I don't blame you for being angry,' he said. 'Yet you have to try to understand. Although my method was indeed questionable, the motives were as pure as driven snow.'

I laughed scornfully. 'There is nothing pure in having your failure determine *my* life!'

He sighed. 'You have time at your disposal?'

'As much as you want.'

'And you are seated comfortably?'

'Perfectly.'

'Then listen to my story. Listen and judge for yourself.'

*

THE STORY OF PETROS PAPACHRISTOS

I cannot pretend to remember as I write now the exact phrasing and expressions my uncle used on that summer afternoon, so many years ago. I have preferred to recreate his narrative in the third person, opting for completeness and coherence. Where memory failed me I consulted his extant correspondence with family and mathematical colleagues as well as the thick, leather-bound volumes of the personal diaries in which he traced the progress of his research.

Petros Papachristos was born in Athens in November 1895. He spent his early childhood in virtual isolation, the first-born of a self-made businessman whose sole concern was his work and a housewife whose sole concern was her husband.

Great loves are often born of loneliness, and this certainly seems to have been true of my uncle's lifelong affair with numbers. He discovered his particular aptitude for calculation early on and it didn't take long for it, for lack of other emotional diversions, to develop into a veritable passion. Even as a little boy, he filled his empty hours doing complicated sums, mostly in his head. By the time his two little brothers' arrival enlivened the household he was already so committed to his pursuit that no changes in family dynamics could distract him.

Petros' school, a religious institution run by French Jesuit brothers, upheld the Order's brilliant tradition in mathematics. Brother Nicolas, his first teacher, immediately recognized his bent and took him under his wing. With his guidance the boy began to cover material way beyond the capabilities of his classmates. Like most Jesuit mathematicians, Brother Nicolas specialized in (the already old-fashioned by that time) classical geometry. He spent his time contriving exercises which, although often ingenious and as a rule monstrously difficult, held no deeper mathematical interest. Petros solved them, as well as any others his teacher culled from the Jesuit maths books, with astonishing ease.

However, his particular passion from the very beginning lay in the Theory of Numbers, a field in which the brothers were not particularly knowledgeable. His undeniable talent together with constant practice since his earliest years had resulted in almost uncanny skills. When Petros, at the age of eleven, heard that every positive integer can be expressed as the sum of four squares, he astonished the good brothers by providing the breakdown of whatever number was suggested after only a few seconds of thought.

'What about 99, Pierre?' they'd ask.

'99 is equal to 8^2 plus 5^2 plus 3^2 plus 1^2,' he'd answer.

'And 290?'

'290 is equal to 12^2 plus 9^2 plus 7^2 plus 4^2.'

'But how on earth can you do it so fast?'

Petros described a method that seemed obvious to him, but to his teachers was difficult to understand and impossible to apply without paper, pencil and sufficient time. The procedure was based on leaps of logic that bypassed intermediate steps of calculation, clear evidence that the boy's mathematical intuition was already developed to an extraordinary degree.

After having taught him more or less everything they knew, when Petros was fifteen or so the brothers found themselves unable to answer their gifted pupil's constant flow of mathematical questions. It was then that the headmaster went to his father. Papachristos *père* may not have had much time for his children, but he knew his duty where the Greek Orthodox faith was concerned. He had enrolled his eldest son in a school run by schismatic foreigners because it held prestige within the social élite to which he aspired to belong. When faced with the headmaster's proposal, however, that his son be sent to a monastery in France in order to further cultivate his mathematical talent, his mind immediately went to proselytism.

'The damn papists want to get their hands on my son,' he thought.

Still, despite lacking higher education, the elder Papachristos was anything but naïve. Knowing from personal experience that one succeeds best in the field of endeavour one has a natural gift for, he had no desire to place any obstacles in his son's natural course. He asked around in the right circles and was informed of the existence, in Germany, of a great mathematician who also happened to belong to the Greek Orthodox persuasion, the renowned Professor Constantin Caratheodory. He immediately wrote to him for an appointment.

Father and son travelled together to Berlin, where Caratheodory received them in his office at the university, dressed like a banker. After a short chat with the father he asked to be left alone with the son. He led him to the blackboard, gave him a piece of chalk and questioned him. Petros solved integrals, calculated the sums of series and proved statements, as prompted. Then, once the esteemed professor had finished his examination, the boy reported his own discoveries: elaborate geometric constructions, complex algebraic identities and, particularly, observations regarding the properties of the integers. One of those was the following:

'Every even number greater than 2 can be written as a sum of two primes.'

'You surely can't prove that,' said the famous mathematician.

'Not yet,' answered Petros, 'although I'm sure it's a

general principle. I've checked it up to 10,000!'

'What about the distribution of the prime numbers?' Caratheodory asked. 'Can you figure a way to calculate how many primes there are lesser than a given number n?'

'No,' answered Petros, 'but as n approaches infinity the quantity gets very close to its ratio by the natural logarithm.'

Caratheodory gasped. 'You must have read that somewhere!'

'No, sir, it just seems a reasonable extrapolation from my tables. Besides, the only books at my school are about geometry.'

The Professor's previously stern expression now gave way to a beaming smile. He called Petros' father inside and told him that to subject his son to two more years of high school would be a complete waste of precious time. Denying his extraordinarily gifted boy the best that mathematical education had to offer would be tantamount, he said, to 'criminal negligence'. Caratheodory would arrange to have Petros immediately admitted to his university – if his guardian consented, of course.

My poor grandfather never had a choice: he had no desire to commit a crime, especially against his first-born.

*

Arrangements were made, and a few months later Petros returned to Berlin and moved into the family home of a business associate of his father's, in Charlottenburg.

During the months preceding the start of the next academic year, the eldest daughter of the house, the eighteen-year-old Isolde, undertook to help the young foreign guest with his German. It being summer, the tutoring sessions were often conducted in secluded corners of the garden. When it got colder, Uncle Petros reminisced with a mellow smile, 'the instruction was continued in bed'.

Isolde was the first and (judging from his narrative) only love my uncle ever had. Their affair was brief and conducted in total secrecy. Their trysts would take place at irregular times in unlikely locations, at noon or midnight or dawn, in the shrubbery or the attic or the wine cellar, wherever and whenever the opportunity for invisibility beckoned: if her father found out, he would string him up by his thumbs, the girl had repeatedly warned her young lover.

For a while, Petros was totally disoriented by love. He became almost indifferent to everything other than his sweetheart, to the point that Caratheodory came to wonder for a while whether he might have been wrong in his original appreciation of the boy's potential. But after a few months of tortuous happiness ('alas, too few,' my uncle said with a sigh), Isolde abandoned the family home and the arms of her boy-lover in order to marry a dashing lieutenant of the Prussian artillery.

Petros was, of course, heartbroken.

If the intensity of his childhood passion for numbers was partly a recompense for the lack of familial tenderness, his immersion into higher mathematics at Berlin University was definitely made all the more complete for the loss of his beloved. The deeper he now delved into its endless ocean of abstract concepts and arcane symbols, the farther he was mercifully removed from the excruciatingly tender memories of 'dearest Isolde'. In fact, in her absence she became 'of much more use' (his words) to Petros. When they had first lain together on her bed (when she had first *thrown* him on to her bed, to be precise) she had softly muttered in his ear that what attracted her to him was his reputation as a *wunderkind*, a little genius. In order to win her heart back, Petros now decided, there could be no half-measures. To impress her at a more mature age he should have to accomplish amazing intellectual feats, nothing short of becoming a Great Mathematician.

But how does one become a Great Mathematician? Simple: by solving a Great Mathematical Problem!

'Which is the most difficult problem in mathematics, Professor?' he asked Caratheodory at their next meeting, trying to feign mere academic curiosity.

'I'll give you the three main contenders,' the sage replied after a moment's hesitation. 'The Riemann Hypothesis, Fermat's Last Theorem and, last but not least, Goldbach's Conjecture, the proof of the observation about every even number being the sum of two primes – one of the great unsolved problems of Number Theory.'

Although by no means yet a firm decision, the first seed of the dream that some day he would prove the Conjecture was apparently planted in his heart by this short exchange. The fact that it stated an observation he had himself made long before he'd heard of Goldbach or Euler made the problem dearer to him. Its formulation had attracted him from the very first. The combination of external simplicity and notorious difficulty pointed of necessity to a profound truth.

At present, however, Caratheodory was not allowing Petros any time for daydreaming.

'Before you can fruitfully embark on original research,' he told him in no uncertain terms, 'you have to acquire a mighty arsenal. You must master to perfection all the tools of the modern mathematician from Analysis, Complex Analysis, Topology and Algebra.'

Even for a young man of his extraordinary talent, this mastery needed time and single-minded attention.

Once he'd received his degree, Caratheodory assigned him for his doctoral dissertation a problem from the theory of differential equations. Petros surprised his master by completing the work in less than a year, and with spectacular success. The method for the solution of a particular variety of equations which he put forth in his thesis (henceforth, the 'Papachristos Method') earned him instant acclaim because of its usefulness in the solution of certain physical problems. Yet – and here I'm quoting him directly – 'it was of no particular mathematical interest, mere calculation of the grocery-bill variety.'

Petros was awarded his doctorate in 1916. Immediately afterwards, his father, worried about the imminent entry of Greece into the mêlée of the Great War, arranged for him to settle for a while in neutral Switzerland. In Zurich, at last a master of his fate, Petros turned to his first and constant love: Numbers.

He sat in on an advanced course at the university, attended lectures and seminars, and spent all his remaining time at the library, devouring books and learned journals. Soon, it became apparent to him that to proceed as fast as possible to the frontiers of knowledge, he had to travel. The three mathematicians doing world-class work in Number Theory at that time were the Englishmen G. H. Hardy and J. E. Littlewood and the extraordinary self-taught Indian genius Srinivasa Ramanujan. All three were at Trinity College, Cambridge.

The war had divided Europe geographically, with England practically cut off from the mainland by patrolling German U-boats. However, Petros' intense desire, combined with his total indifference to the danger involved as well as his more than ample means, soon got him to his destination.

'I arrived in England still a beginner,' he told me, 'but left it, three years later, an expert number theorist.'

Indeed, the time in Cambridge was his essential preparation for the long, hard years that followed. He had no official academic appointment, but his – or rather his father's – financial situation allowed him the luxury of subsisting without one. He settled down in a small boarding-house next to the Bishop Hostel, where Srinivasa Ramanujan was staying at the time. Soon, he was on friendly terms with him and together they attended G. H. Hardy's lectures.

Hardy embodied the prototype of the modern research mathematician. A true master of his craft, he approached Number Theory with brilliant clarity, using the most sophisticated mathematical methods to tackle its central problems, many of which were, like Goldbach's Conjecture, of deceptive external simplicity. At his lectures, Petros learned the techniques which would prove necessary to his work and began to develop the profound mathematical intuition required for advanced research. He was a fast learner, and soon he began to chart out the labyrinth into which he was fated soon to enter.

Yet, although Hardy was crucial to his mathematical development, it was his contact with Ramanujan that provided him with inspiration.

'Oh, he was a totally unique phenomenon,' Petros told me with a sigh. 'As Hardy used to say, in terms of mathematical capability Ramanujan was at the absolute zenith; he was made of the same cloth as Archimedes, Newton and Gauss – it was even conceivable that he surpassed them. However, the near-total lack of formal mathematical training during his formative years had for all practical purposes condemned him never to be able to fulfil anything but a tiny fraction of his genius.'

To watch Ramanujan do mathematics was a humbling experience. Awe and amazement were the only possible reactions to his uncanny ability to conceive, in sudden flashes or epiphanies, the most inconceivably complex formulas and identities. (To the great frustration of the ultra-rationalist Hardy, he would often claim that his beloved Hindu goddess Namakiri had revealed these to him in a dream.) One was led to wonder: if the extreme poverty into which he had been born had not deprived Ramanujan of the education granted to the average well-fed Western student, what heights might he have attained?

One day, Petros timidly brought up with him the subject of Goldbach's Conjecture. He was purposely tentative, concerned that he might awaken his interest in the problem.

Ramanujan's answer came as an unpleasant surprise. 'I have a hunch, you know, that the Conjecture may not apply for some very very big numbers.'

Petros was thunderstruck. Could it possibly be? Coming from him, this comment couldn't be taken lightly. At the first opportunity, after a lecture, he approached Hardy and repeated it to him, trying at the same time to appear rather blasé about the matter.

Hardy smiled a cunning little smile. 'Good old Ramanujan has been known to have some wonderful "hunches",' he said, 'and his intuitive powers are phenomenal. Still, unlike His Holiness the Pope, he lays no claim to infallibility.'

Then Hardy eyed Petros intently, a gleam of irony in his eyes. 'But tell me, my dear fellow, why this sudden interest in Goldbach's Conjecture?'

Petros mumbled a banality about his 'general interest in the problem' and then asked, as innocently as possible: 'Is there anyone working on it?'

'You mean actually trying to prove it?' said Hardy. 'Why no – to attempt to do so directly would be sheer folly!'

The warning did not scare him off; on the contrary it pointed out the course he should follow. The meaning of Hardy's words was clear: the straightforward, so-called 'elementary' approach to the problem was doomed to failure. The right way lay in the oblique 'analytic' method that, following the recent great success of the French mathematicians Hadamard and de la Vallée-Poussin with it, had become *tres à la mode* in Number Theory. Soon, he was totally immersed in its study.

There was a time, in Cambridge, before he made the final decision about his life's work, when Petros seriously considered devoting his energies to a different problem altogether. This came about as a result of his unexpected entry into the Hardy–Littlewood–Ramanujan inner circle.

During those wartime years, J. E. Littlewood had not been spending much time around the university. He would show up every now and then for a rare lecture or a meeting and then disappear once again to God knows where, an aura of mystery surrounding his activities. Petros had yet to meet him and so was greatly surprised when, one day in early 1917, Littlewood sought him out at the boarding-house.

'Are you Petros Papachristos from Berlin?' he asked him, after a handshake and a cautious smile. 'Constantin Caratheodory's student?'

'I am the one, yes,' answered Petros perplexed.

Littlewood appeared slightly ill at ease as he went on to explain: he was at that time in charge of a team of scientists doing ballistics research for the Royal Artillery as part of the war effort. Military intelligence had recently alerted them to the fact that the enemy's high accuracy of fire in the Western Front was thought to be the result of an innovative new technique of calculation, called the 'Papachristos Method'.

'I'm sure you wouldn't have any objection to sharing your discovery with His Majesty's Government, old chap,' Littlewood concluded. 'After all, Greece is on our side.'

Petros was at first dismayed, fearing he would be obliged to waste valuable time with problems that held no more interest for him. That didn't prove necessary, though. The text of his dissertation, which he luckily had with him, contained more than enough mathematics for the needs of the Royal Artillery. Littlewood was doubly pleased since the Papachristos Method, apart from its immediate usefulness to the war effort, significantly lightened his own load, giving him more time to devote to his main mathematical interests.

So: rather than side-tracking him, Petros' earlier success with differential equations provided his entry into one of the most renowned partnerships in the history of mathematics. Littlewood was delighted to learn that the heart of his gifted Greek colleague belonged, as did his, to Number Theory, and soon he invited him to join him on a visit to Hardy's rooms. The three of them talked mathematics for hours on end. During this, and at all their subsequent meetings, both Littlewood and Petros avoided any mention of what had originally brought them together; Hardy was a fanatical pacifist and strongly opposed to the use of scientific discoveries in facilitating warfare.

After the Armistice, when Littlewood returned to Cambridge full-time, he asked Petros to collaborate with him and Hardy on a paper they had originally begun with Ramanujan. (The poor fellow was by now seriously ill and spending most of his time in a sanatorium.) At that time, the two great number theorists had turned their efforts to the Riemann Hypothesis, the epicentre of most of the unproven central results of the analytic approach. A demonstration of Bernhard Riemann's insight on the zeros of his 'zeta function' would create a positive domino effect, resulting in the proof of countless fundamental theorems of Number Theory. Petros accepted their proposal (which ambitious young mathematician wouldn't?) and the three of them jointly published, in 1918 and 1919, two papers – the two that my friend Sammy Epstein had found under his name in the bibliographical index.

Ironically, these would also be his last published work.

After this first collaboration Hardy, an uncompromising judge of mathematical talent, proposed to Petros that he accept a fellowship at Trinity and settle in Cambridge to become a permanent part of their élite team.

Petros asked for time to think it over. Of course, the proposal was enormously flattering and the prospect of continuing their collaboration had, at first glance, great appeal. Continued association with Hardy and Littlewood would no doubt result in more fine work, work that would assure his rapid ascent in the scientific community. In addition, Petros liked the two men. Being around them was not only agreeable but enormously stimulating. The very air they breathed was infused with brilliant, important mathematics.

Yet, despite all this, the prospect of staying on filled him with apprehension.

If he remained in Cambridge he would steer a predictable course. He would produce good, even exceptional work, but his progress would be determined by Hardy and Littlewood. Their problems would become his own and, what's worse, their fame would inevitably outshine his. If they did manage eventually to prove the Riemann Hypothesis (as Petros hoped they would) it would certainly be a feat of great import, a world-shaking achievement of momentous proportions. But would it be *his*? In fact, would even the third of the credit due to him by right be truly his own? Wasn't it likelier that his part in the achievement would be eclipsed by the fame of his two illustrious colleagues?

Anybody who claims that scientists – even the purest of the pure, the most abstract, high-flying mathematicians – are motivated exclusively by the Pursuit of Truth for the Good of Mankind, either has no idea what he's talking about or is blatantly lying. Although the more spiritually inclined members of the scientific community may indeed be indifferent to material gains, there isn't a single one among them who isn't mainly driven by ambition and a strong competitive urge. (Of course, in the case of a great mathematical achievement the field of contestants is necessarily limited – in fact, the greater the achievement the more limited the field. The rivals for the trophy being the select few, the cream of the crop, competition becomes a veritable *gigantomachia*, a battle of giants.) A mathematician's declared intention, when embarking on an important research endeavour, may indeed be the discovery of Truth, yet the stuff of his daydreams is Glory.

My uncle was no exception – this he admitted to me with full candour when recounting his tale. After Berlin and the disappointment with 'dearest Isolde' he had sought in mathematics a great, almost transcendent success, a total triumph that would bring him world fame and (he hoped) the cold-hearted *Mädchen* begging on her knees. And to be complete, this triumph should be exclusively his own, not parcelled out and divided into two or three.

Also weighing against his staying on in Cambridge was the question of time. Mathematics, you see, is a young man's game. It is one of the few human endeavours (in this very similar to sports) where youth is a necessary requirement for greatness. Petros, like every young mathematician, knew the depressing statistics: hardly ever in the history of the field had a great discovery been made by a man over thirty-five or forty. Riemann had died at thirty-nine, Niels Henrik Abel at twenty-seven and Evariste Galois at a mere tragic twenty, yet their names were inscribed in gold in the pages of mathematical history, the 'Riemann Zeta Function', 'Abelian Integrals' and 'Galois Groups' an undying legacy for future mathematicians. Euler and Gauss may have worked and produced theorems into advanced old age, yet their fundamental discoveries had been made in their early youth. In any other field, at twenty-four Petros would be a promising beginner with years and years and years of rich creative opportunities ahead of him. In mathematics, however, he was already at the peak of his powers.

He estimated that he had, with luck, at the most ten years in which to dazzle humanity (as well as 'dearest Isolde') with a great, magnificent, colossal achievement. After that time, sooner or later, his strength would begin to wane. Technique and knowledge would hopefully survive, yet the spark required to set off the majestic fireworks, the inventive brilliance and the sprightly spirit-of-attack necessary for a truly Great Discovery (the dream of proving Goldbach's Conjecture was by now increasingly occupying his thoughts) would fade, if not altogether disappear.

After not-too-long deliberation he decided that Hardy and Littlewood would have to continue on their course alone.

From now on he couldn't afford to waste a single day. His most productive years were ahead of him, irresistibly urging him forward. He should immediately set to work on his problem.

As to which problem this would be: the only candidates he had ever considered were the three great open questions that Caratheodory had casually mentioned a few years back – nothing smaller would suit his ambition. Of these, the Riemann Hypothesis was already in Hardy and Littlewood's hands and scientific *savoir-faire*, as well as prudence, deemed that he leave it alone. As to Fermat's Last Theorem, the methods traditionally employed in attacking it were too algebraic for his taste. So, the choice was really quite simple: the vehicle by which he would realize his dream of fame and immortality could not be other than Goldbach's humble-sounding Conjecture.

The offer of the Chair of Analysis at Munich University had come a bit earlier, at just the right moment. It was an ideal position. The rank of full professor, an indirect reward for the military usefulness of the Papachristos Method to the Kaiser's army, would grant Petros freedom from an excessive teaching load and provide financial independence from his father, should he ever get the notion of attempting to lure him back to Greece and the family business. In Munich, he would be practically free of all irrelevant obligations. His few lecture hours would not be too much of an intrusion on his private time; on the contrary they could provide a constant, living link with the analytic techniques he would be using in his research.

The last thing Petros wanted was to have others intruding on his problem. Leaving Cambridge, he had deliberately covered his tracks with a smokescreen. Not only did he not disclose to Hardy and Littlewood the fact that he would henceforth be working on Goldbach's Conjecture, but he led them to believe that he would be continuing work on their beloved Riemann Hypothesis. And in this too, Munich was ideal: its School of Mathematics was not a particularly famous one, like that of Berlin or the near-legendary Göttingen, and thus it was safely removed from the great centres of mathematical gossip and inquisitiveness

In the summer of 1919, Petros settled in a dark second-floor apartment (he believed that too much light is incompatible with absolute concentration) at a short walk from the university. He got to know his new colleagues at the School of Mathematics and made arrangements regarding the teaching programme with his assistants, most of them his seniors. Then he set up his working environment in his home, where distractions could be kept to a minimum. His housekeeper, a quiet middle-aged Jewish lady widowed in the recent war, was told in the most unambiguous manner that once he had entered his study he was not to be disturbed, for any reason on earth.

After more than forty years, my uncle still remembered with exceptional clarity the day when he began his research.

The sun had not yet risen when he sat at his desk, picked up his thick fountain pen and wrote on a clean, crisp piece of white paper:

STATEMENT: *Every even number greater than 2 is the sum of two primes.*

PROOF: *Assume the above statement to be false. Then, there is an integer n such that 2n cannot be expressed as the sum of two primes, i.e. for every prime p < 2n, 2n-p is composite . . .*

After a few months of hard work, he began to get a sense of the true dimensions of the problem and sign-posted the most obvious dead-ends. He could now map out a main strategy for his approach and identify some of the intermediate results that he needed to prove. Following the military analogy, he referred to these as the 'hills of strategic importance that had to be taken before mounting the final attack on the Conjecture itself'.

Of course, his whole approach was based on the analytic method.

In both its algebraic and its analytic versions, Number Theory has the same object, namely to study the properties of the *integers*, the positive whole numbers 1, 2,

3, 4, 5 . . . etc. as well as their interrelations. As physical research is often the study of the elementary particles of matter, so are many of the central problems of higher arithmetic reduced to those of the *primes* (integers that have no divisors other than 1 and themselves, like 2, 3, 5, 7, 11 . . .), the irreducible quanta of the number system.

The Ancient Greeks, and after them the great mathematicians of the European Enlightenment such as Pierre de Fermat, Leonard Euler and Carl Friedrich Gauss, had discovered a host of interesting theorems concerning the primes (of these we mentioned earlier Euclid's proof of their infinitude). Yet, until the middle of the nineteenth century, the most fundamental truths about them remained beyond the reach of mathematicians.

Chief among these were two: their 'distribution' (i.e. the quantity of primes less than a given integer n), and the pattern of their succession, the elusive formula by which, given a certain prime p_n, one could determine the next, p_{n+1}. Often (maybe infinitely often, according to a hypothesis) primes come separated by only two integers, in pairs such as 5 and 7, 11 and 13, 41 and 43, or 9857 and 9859.* Yet, in other instances, two consecutive primes can be separated by

* The largest such pair known today is almost inconceivably enormous: $83535^{39014} +/-1$.

hundreds or thousands or millions of non-prime integers – in fact, it is extremely simple to prove that for any given integer k, one can find a succession of k integers that doesn't contain a single prime.*

The seeming absence of any ascertained organizing principle in the distribution or the succession of the primes had bedevilled mathematicians for centuries and given Number Theory much of its fascination. Here was a great mystery indeed, worthy of the most exalted intelligence: since the primes are the building blocks of the integers and the integers the basis of our logical understanding of the cosmos, how is it possible that their form is not determined by law? Why isn't 'divine geometry' apparent in their case?

The analytic theory of numbers was born in 1837, with Dirichlet's striking proof of the infinitude of primes in arithmetic progressions. Yet it didn't reach its peak until the end of the century. Some years before Dirichlet, Carl Friedrich Gauss had arrived at a good guess of an 'asymptotic' formula (i.e. an approximation, getting better and better as n grows) of the number of primes less than a certain integer n. Yet neither he nor anyone after him had been able to suggest a

* Let k be a given integer. The set $(k + 2)! + 2, (k + 2)! + 3, (k + 2)! + 4 \ldots (k + 2)! + (k + 1), (k + 2)! + (k + 2)$ contains k integers none of which is prime, since each is divisible by $2, 3, 4 \ldots, k + 1, k + 2$ respectively. (The symbol $k!$, also known as 'k factorial', means the product of all the integers from 1 to k.)

hint of a proof. Then in 1859, Bernhard Riemann introduced an infinite sum in the plane of complex numbers,* ever since known as the 'Riemann Zeta Function', which promised to be an extremely useful new tool. To use it effectively, however, number theorists had to abandon their traditional, algebraic (so-called 'elementary') techniques and resort to the methods of Complex Analysis, i.e. the infinitesimal calculus applied to the plane of complex numbers.

A few decades later, when Hadamard and de la Vallée-Poussin managed to prove Gauss's asymptotic formula using the Riemann Zeta Function (a result henceforth known as the Prime Number Theorem) the analytic approach suddenly seemed to become the magic key to the innermost secrets of Number Theory.

It was at the time of this high tide of hope in the analytic approach that Petros began his work on Goldbach's Conjecture.

After spending the initial few months familiarizing himself with the dimensions of his problem, he decided he would proceed through the Theory of Partitions (the different ways of writing an integer as a sum), another application of the analytic method. Apart from the central theorem in the field, by Hardy

* Numbers of the form a + bi, where a, b are real numbers and i is the 'imaginary' square root of -1.

and Ramanujan, there also existed a hypothesis by the latter (another of his famous 'hunches') which Petros hoped would become a crucial stepping stone to the Conjecture itself – if only he managed to prove it.

He wrote to Littlewood, asking as discreetly as possible whether there had been any more recent developments in this matter, his question purportedly expressing 'a colleague's interest'. Littlewood reported in the negative, also sending him Hardy's new book, *Some Famous Problems of Number Theory*. In it, there was a proof of sorts of what is known as the Second or 'other' Conjecture of Goldbach.* This so-called proof, however, had a fundamental lacuna: its validity relied on the (unproven) Riemann Hypothesis. Petros read this and smiled a superior smile. Hardy was becoming pretty desperate, publishing results based on unproven premises! Goldbach's main Conjecture, *the* Conjecture, as far as he was concerned, was not even given lip service; his problem was safe.

Petros conducted his research in total secrecy, and the deeper his probing led him into the *terra incognita* defined by the Conjecture, the more zealously he covered his tracks. For his more curious colleagues he had the same decoy answer that he'd used with Hardy and Littlewood: he was building on the work he had done

* This states that any odd number greater than 5 is the sum of three primes.

with them in Cambridge, continuing their joint research on the Riemann Hypothesis. With time, he became cautious to the point of paranoia. In order to avoid his colleagues' drawing conclusions from the items he withdrew from the library, he began to find ways of disguising his requests. He would protect the book he really wanted by including it in a list of three or four irrelevant ones, or he would ask for an article in a scientific journal only in order to get his hands on the issue that also contained *another* article, the one he really wanted, to be perused far from inquiring eyes in the total privacy of his study.

In the spring of that year, Petros received an additional short communication from Hardy, announcing Srinivasa Ramanujan's death of tuberculosis, at the age of thirty-two, in a slum neighbourhood of Madras. His first reaction to the sad news perplexed and even distressed him. Under a surface layer of sorrow for the loss of the extraordinary mathematician and the gentle, humble, sweet-spoken friend, Petros felt deep inside a wild joy that this phenomenal brain was no longer in the arena of Number Theory.

You see, he had feared no one else. His two most qualified rivals, Hardy and Littlewood, were too involved with the Riemann Hypothesis to think seriously about Goldbach's Conjecture. As to David Hilbert, generally acknowledged to be the world's greatest living mathematician, or Jacques Hadamard, the only other number theorist to be reckoned with, both were by now really no more than esteemed veterans – their almost sixty years were tantamount to advanced old age for creative mathematicians. But he *had* feared Ramanujan. His unique intellect was the only force he considered capable of purloining his prize. Despite the doubts he had expressed to Petros about the general validity of the Conjecture, should Ramanujan ever have decided to focus his genius on the problem . . . . Who knows, maybe he would have been able to prove it despite himself; maybe his dear goddess Namakiri would have offered the solution to him in a dream, all neatly written out in Sanskrit on a roll of parchment!

Now, with his death, there was no longer any real danger of someone arriving at the solution before Petros.

Still, when he was invited by the great School of Mathematics at Göttingen to deliver a memorial lecture on Ramanujan's contribution to Number Theory, he carefully avoided mentioning his work on Partitions, lest anyone be inspired to look into its possible connections with Goldbach's Conjecture.

In the late summer of 1922 (as it happened, on the very same day that his country was ravaged by the news of the destruction of Smyrna) Petros was suddenly faced with his first great dilemma.

The occasion was a particularly happy one: while taking a long walk on the shore of the Speichersee, he arrived by way of a sudden illumination, following months of excruciating work, at an amazing insight. He sat down in a small beer-garden and scribbled it in the notebook he always carried with him. Then he took the first train back to Munich and spent the hours of dusk till dawn at his desk, working out the details and going over his syllogism carefully, again and again. When he was finished he felt for the second time in his life (the first had to do with Isolde) a feeling of total fulfilment, absolute happiness. He had managed to prove Ramanujan's hypothesis!

In the first years of his work on the Conjecture, he had accumulated quite a few interesting intermediate results, so-called 'lemmas' or smaller theorems, some of which were of unquestionable interest, ample material for several worthwhile publications. Yet he had never been seriously tempted to make these public. Although they were respectable enough, none of them could qualify as an important discovery, even by the esoteric standards of the number theorist.

But now things were different.

The problem he had solved on his afternoon walk

by the Speichersee was of particular importance. As regarded his work on the Conjecture it was of course still an intermediate step, not his ultimate goal. Nevertheless, it was a deep, pioneering theorem in its own right, one which opened new vistas in the Theory of Numbers. It shed a new light on the question of Partitions, applying the previous Hardy–Ramanujan theorem in a way that no one had suspected, let alone demonstrated, before. Undoubtedly, its publication would secure him recognition in the mathematical world much greater than that achieved by his method for solving differential equations. In fact, it would probably catapult him to the first ranks of the small but select international community of number theorists, practically on the same level as its great stars, Hadamard, Hardy and Littlewood.

By making his discovery public, he would also be opening the way into the problem to other mathematicians who would build on it by discovering new results and expand the limits of the field in a way a lone researcher, however brilliant, could scarcely hope. The results they would achieve would, in turn, aid him in his pursuit of the proof to the Conjecture. In other words, by publishing the 'Papachristos Partition Theorem' (modesty of course obliged him to wait for his colleagues formally to give it this title) he would be acquiring a legion of assistants in his work. Unfortunately there was another side to this coin: one of the new unpaid (also unasked for) assistants might conceivably stumble upon a better way to apply his theorem and manage, God forbid, to prove Goldbach's Conjecture before him.

He didn't have to deliberate long. The danger far outweighed the benefit. He wouldn't publish. The 'Papachristos Partitions Theorem' would remain for the time being his private, well-guarded secret.

Reminiscing for my benefit, Uncle Petros marked this decision as a turning point in his life. From then onwards, he said, difficulties began to pile upon difficulties.

By withholding publication of his first truly important contribution to mathematics, he had placed himself under double time-pressure. In addition to the constant, gnawing anxiety of days and weeks and months and years passing without his having achieved the desired final goal, he now also had to worry that someone might arrive at his discovery independently and steal his glory.

The official successes he had achieved until then (a discovery named after him and a university chair) were no mean feats. But time counts differently for mathematicians. He was now at the absolute peak of his powers, in a creative prime that couldn't last long.

This was the time to make his great discovery – if he had it in him to make it at all.

Living as he did a life of near-total isolation, there was no one to ease his pressures.

The loneliness of the researcher doing original mathematics is unlike any other. In a very real sense of the word, he lives in a universe that is totally inaccessible, both to the greater public and to his immediate environment. Even those closest to him cannot partake of his joys and his sorrows in any significant way, since it is all but impossible for them to understand their content.

The only community to which the creative mathematician can truly belong is that of his peers; but from that Petros had wilfully cut himself off. During his first years at Munich he had submitted occasionally to the traditional academic hospitality towards newcomers. When he accepted an invitation, however, it was sheer agony to act with a semblance of normality, behave agreeably and make small talk. He had constantly to curb his tendency to lose himself in number-theoretical thoughts, and fight his frequent impulses to make a mad dash for home and his desk, in the grip of a hunch that required immediate attention. Fortunately, either as a result of his increasingly frequent refusals or his obvious discomfort and awkwardness on those occasions when he did attend social functions, invitations gradually grew fewer and fewer and in the end, to his great relief, ceased altogether.

I don't need to add that he never married. The rationale he gave me for this, by which getting married to another woman would mean being unfaithful to his great love, 'dearest Isolde', was of course no more than an excuse. In truth, he was very much aware that his lifestyle did not allow for the presence of another person. His preoccupation with his research was ceaseless. Goldbach's Conjecture demanded him whole: his body, his soul and all of his time.

In the summer of 1925, Petros proved a second important result, which in combination with the 'Partitions Theorem' opened up a new perspective on many of the classical problems of prime numbers. According to his own, exceedingly fair and well-informed opinion, the work he had done constituted a veritable breakthrough. The temptation to publish was now overwhelming. It tortured him for weeks – once again, though, he managed to resist it. Again, he decided in favour of keeping his secret to himself, lest it open the way to unwelcome intruders. No intermediate result, no matter how important, could sidetrack him from his original aim. He would prove Goldbach's Conjecture or be damned!

In November of that year he turned thirty, an

emblematic age for the research mathematician, practically the first step into middle age.

The sword of Damocles, whose presence Petros had merely sensed all these years hanging in the darkness somewhere high above him (it was labelled: 'The Waning of his Creative Powers') now became almost visible. More and more, as he sat hunched over his papers, he could feel its hovering menace. The invisible hourglass measuring out his creative prime became a constant presence at the back of his mind, driving him into bouts of dread and anxiety. During his every waking moment, he was pestered by the worry that he might already be moving away from the apex of his intellectual prowess. Questions buzzed in his mind like mosquitoes: would he be having any more breakthroughs of the same order as the two first important results? Had the inevitable decline, perhaps unbeknown to him, already started? Every little instance of forgetfulness, every tiny slip in a calculation, every short lapse in concentration, brought the ominous refrain: *Have I passed my prime?*

A brief visit at about this time from his family (already described to me by my father), whom he hadn't seen in years, was considered by him a gross, violent intrusion. The little time he spent with his parents and younger brothers he felt was stolen from his work, and every moment away from his desk for their benefit he perceived as a small dose of mathematical suicide. By the end of their stay he was inordinately frustrated.

Not wasting time had become a veritable obsession, to the point where he obliterated from his life any activity that was not directly related to Goldbach's Conjecture – all except the two he couldn't reduce beyond a certain minimum, teaching and sleep. Yet he now got less sleep than he needed. Constant anxiety had brought insomnia with it, and this was aggravated by his excessive consumption of coffee, the fuel on which mathematicians run. With time, the constant preoccupation with the Conjecture made it impossible for him to relax. Falling or staying asleep became increasingly difficult and often he had to resort to sleeping pills. Occasional use gradually became steady and doses began to increase alarmingly, to the point of dependency, and this without the accompanying beneficial effect.

At about this time, a totally unexpected boost to his spirits came in the unlikely form of a dream. Despite his total disbelief in the supernatural, Petros viewed it as prophetic, a definite omen straight from Mathematical Heaven.

It is not unusual for scientists totally immersed in a difficult problem to carry on their preoccupations into sleep; and although Petros was never honoured by nocturnal visitations from Ramanujan's Namakiri or any other revelatory deity (a fact that should not surprise us, considering his entrenched agnosticism), after the first year or so of his immersion in the Conjecture he began to have the occasional mathematical dream. In fact, his early visions of amorous bliss in the arms of 'dearest Isolde' became less frequent over time, giving their place to dreams of the Even Numbers, which appeared personified as couples of identical twins. They were involved in intricate, unearthly dumbshows, a chorus to the Primes, who were peculiar hermaphrodite, semi-human beings. Unlike the speechless Even Numbers, the Primes often chattered among themselves, usually in an unintelligible language, at the same time executing bizarre dance-steps. (By his admission, this dream choreography was most likely inspired by a production of Stravinsky's *Rite of Spring* that Petros had attended during his early years in Munich, when he still had time for such vanities.) On rare occasions the singular creatures spoke and then only in classical Greek – perhaps as a tribute to Euclid, who had awarded them infinitude. Even when their utterances made some linguistic sense, however, the content was mathematically either trivial or nonsensical. Petros specifically recalled one such: *hapantes protoi perittoi*, which means 'All prime numbers are odd', an obviously false statement. (By a different reading of the word *perittoi*, however, it could also mean 'All prime numbers are useless', an interpretation which, interestingly, completely escaped my uncle's attention.)

Yet in a few rare instances there was something of substance in his dreams. He could deduce from the protagonists' sayings helpful hints that steered his research towards interesting, unexplored paths.[*]

The dream that lifted his spirits came a few nights after he had proved his second important result. It was not directly mathematical, but laudatory, consisting of no more than a single image, a sparkling *tableau vivant*, but of such unearthly beauty! Leonard Euler was on the one side and Christian Goldbach (though he'd never seen a portrait, he immediately knew it to be him) on the other. The two men jointly held, from the

---

[*] In his seminal work *The Nature of Mathematical Discovery*, Henri Poincaré demolishes the myth of the mathematician as a totally rational being. With examples drawn from history, as well as from his own research experience, he places special emphasis on the role of the unconscious in research. Often, he says, great discoveries happen unexpectedly, in a flash of revelation that comes in a moment of repose – of course, these can occur only to minds that are otherwise prepared through endless months or years of conscious work. It is in this aspect of the workings of a mathematician's mind that revelatory dreams can play an important role, sometimes providing the route through which the unconscious announces its conclusions to the conscious mind.

sides, a golden wreath over the head of the central figure, which was none other than himself, Petros Papachristos. The triad was bathed in a nimbus of blinding light.

The dream's message could not be clearer: the proof of Goldbach's Conjecture would be ultimately his.

Spurred by the glorious spirit of this vision, his mood swung back to optimism and he coaxed himself onwards with added zest. Now, he should concentrate all his powers on his research. He could afford absolutely no distractions.

The painful gastrointestinal symptoms he had been having for some time (most of them by some strange coincidence occurring at times when they interfered with his university duties), a result of the constant, self-imposed pressure, gave him the pretext he needed. Armed with the opinion of a specialist, he went to see the Director of the School of Mathematics and requested a two-year, unpaid leave of absence.

The Director, an insignificant mathematician but a ferocious bureaucrat, was apparently waiting for an occasion to level with Professor Papachristos.

'I have read your doctor's recommendation, Herr Professor,' he said in a sour tone. 'Apparently you suffer – like many in our School – from gastritis, a condition that is not exactly terminal. Isn't a two-year leave rather excessive?'

'Well, Herr Director,' mumbled Petros, 'I also happen to be at a critical point in my research. While on my two-year leave I can complete it.'

The Director appeared genuinely surprised. '*Research*? Oh, I had no idea! You see, the fact that you haven't published anything during all your years with us had led your colleagues to think that you were scientifically inactive.'

Petros knew the next question was inevitable:

'By the way, what exactly is it you are researching, Herr Professor?'

'We-ell,' he replied meekly, 'I am investigating certain questions in Number Theory.'

The Director, an eminently practical man, considered Number Theory, a field notorious for the inapplicability of its results to the physical sciences, a complete waste of time. His own interest lay in differential equations and, years back, he had hoped that the addition of the inventor of the Papachristos Method to the faculty would perhaps put his own name on some joint publications. This, of course, had never come about.

'You mean Number Theory *in general*, Herr Professor?'

Petros suffered the ensuing cat-and-mouse game for a while, trying desperately to prevaricate concerning his real object. When, however, he realized he had not the slightest hope unless he convinced the Director of the importance of his work, he revealed the truth.

'I'm working on Goldbach's Conjecture, Herr Director. But *please* don't tell anyone!'

The Director appeared startled. 'Oh? And how are you progressing?'

'Quite well, actually.'

'Which means you have arrived at some very interesting intermediate results. Am I right?'

Petros felt as if he were walking on a tightrope. How much could he safely reveal?

'Well ... er ...' He was fidgeting in his seat, sweating profusely. 'In fact, Herr Director, I believe I'm only one step away from the proof. If you would let me have my two years of unpaid leave, I will try to complete it.'

The Director knew Goldbach's Conjecture – who didn't? Despite the fact that it belonged to the cloud-cuckoo-land world of Number Theory it had the advantage of being an exceedingly famous problem. A success by Professor Papachristos (he was reputed to have, after all, a first-class mind) would definitely be to the great benefit of the university, the School of Mathematics and of course himself, its director. After pondering the matter for a while, he gave him a big smile and declared he wasn't unfavourable to the request.

When Petros went to thank him and say goodbye, the Director was all smiles.

'Good luck with the Conjecture, Herr Professor. I expect you back with great results!'

Having secured his two-year period of grace, he moved to the outskirts of Innsbruck, in the Austrian Tyrol, where he had rented a small cottage. As a forwarding address he left only the local *poste restante*. In his new, temporary abode he was a complete stranger. Here, he needn't fear even the minor distractions of Munich, a chance encounter with an acquaintance in the street or the solicitude of his housekeeper, whom he left behind to look after the empty apartment. His isolation would remain absolutely inviolate.

During his stay in Innsbruck, there was a development in Petros' life that turned out to have a beneficial effect both on his mood and, as a consequence, on his work: he discovered chess.

One evening, while out for his habitual walk, he stopped for a hot drink at a coffee-house, which happened to be the meeting-place of the local club. He had been taught the rules of chess and played a few games as a child, yet he remained to that day totally unaware of its profundity. Now, as he sipped his cocoa, his attention was caught by the game in progress at the next table and he followed it through with increasing interest. The next evening his footsteps led him to the same place, and the day after that as well. At first through mere observation, he gradually began to grasp the fascinating logic of the game.

After a few visits, he accepted a challenge to play. He lost, which was an irritant to his antagonistic nature, particularly so when he learned that his opponent was a cattle-herder by occupation. He stayed up that night, recreating the moves in his mind, trying to pinpoint his mistakes. The next evenings he lost a few more games, but then he won one and felt immense joy, a feeling that spurred him on towards more victories.

Gradually, he became a habitué of the coffee-house and joined the chess club. One of the members told him about the huge volume of accumulated wisdom on the subject of the game's first moves, also known as 'opening theory'. Petros borrowed a basic book and bought the chess set that he was still using in his old age, at his house in Ekali. He'd always kept late nights, but in Innsbruck it wasn't due to Goldbach. With the pieces set out in front of him and the book in hand, he spent the hours before sleep teaching himself the basic openings, the 'Ruy Lopez', the 'King's' and 'Queen's Gambits', the 'Sicilian Defence'.

Armed with some theoretical knowledge he proceeded to win more and more often, to his huge satisfaction. Indeed, displaying the fanaticism of the recent convert, he went overboard for a while, spending time on the game which belonged to his mathematical research, going to the coffee-house earlier and earlier, even turning to his chessboard during the daylight hours to analyse the previous day's games. However, he soon disciplined himself and restricted his chess activity to his nightly outing and an hour or so of study (an opening, or a famous game) before bedtime. Despite this, by the time he left Innsbruck he was the undisputed local champion.

The change brought about in Petros' life by chess was considerable. From the moment he had first dedicated himself to proving Goldbach's Conjecture, almost a decade earlier, he had hardly ever relaxed from his work. However, for a mathematician to spend time away from the problem at hand is essential. Mentally to digest the work accomplished and process its results at an unconscious level, the mind needs leisure as well as exertion. Invigorating as the investigation of mathematical concepts can be to a calm intellect, it can become intolerable when the brain is overcome by weariness, exhausted by incessant effort.

Of the mathematicians of his acquaintance, each had his own way of relaxing. For Caratheodory it was his administrative duties at Berlin University. With his colleagues at the School of Mathematics it varied: for family men it was usually the family; for some it was sports; for some, collecting or the theatrical performances, concerts and other cultural events that were on constant offer at Munich. None of these, however, suited Petros – none engaged him sufficiently to provide distraction from his research. At some point he tried reading detective stories, but after he'd exhausted the exploits of the ultra-rationalist Sherlock Holmes he found nothing else to hold his attention. As for his long afternoon walks, they definitely did not count as relaxation. While his body moved, whether in the countryside or the city, by a serene lakeside or on a busy pavement, his mind was totally preoccupied with the Conjecture, the walking itself being no more than a way to focus on his research.

So, chess seemed to have been sent to him from heaven. Being by its nature a cerebral game, it has concentration as a necessary requirement. Unless matched with a much inferior opponent, and sometimes even then, the player's attention can only wander at a cost. Petros now immersed himself in the recorded encounters between the great players (Steinitz, Alekhine, Capablanca) with a concentration known to him only from his mathematical studies. While trying to defeat Innsbruck's better players he discovered that it was possible to take total leave of Goldbach, even if only for a few hours. Faced with a strong opponent he realized, to his utter amazement, that for a few hours he could think of nothing but chess. The effect was invigorating. The morning after a challenging game he would tackle the Conjecture with a clear and refreshed mind, new perspectives and connections emerging, just as he'd begun to fear that he was drying up.

The relaxing effect of chess also helped Petros to wean himself from sleeping pills. From then on, if some night he were overcome by fruitless anxiety connected with the Conjecture, his tired brain twisting and wandering in endless mathematical mazes, he would get up from bed, seat himself before the chessboard and go over the moves of an interesting game. Immersing himself in it, he would temporarily forget his mathematics, his eyelids would grow heavy and he would sleep like a baby in his armchair till morning.

Before his two years of unpaid leave were up, Petros took a momentous decision: he would publish his two important discoveries, the 'Papachristos Partition Theorem' and the other one.

This, it must be stressed, was not because he had now decided to be content with less. There was no defeatism whatsoever concerning his ultimate aim of proving Goldbach's Conjecture. In Innsbruck, Petros had calmly reviewed the state of knowledge on his problem. He'd gone over the results arrived at by other mathematicians before him and also he'd analysed the course of his own research. Retracing his steps and coolly assessing his achievement to date, two things became obvious: a) His two theorems on Partitions were important results in their own right, and b) They brought him no closer to the proof of the Conjecture – his initial plan of attack had not yielded results.

The intellectual peace he had achieved in Innsbruck resulted in a fundamental insight: the fallacy in his approach lay in the adoption of the analytic approach. He realized now that he had been led astray by the success of Hadamard and de la Vallée-Poussin in proving the Prime Number Theorem and also, especially, by Hardy's authority. In other words, he had been misled by the demands of mathematical fashion (oh yes, such a thing does exist!), demands that have no greater right to be considered Mathematical Truth than the annually changing whims of the gurus of *haute couture* do to be regarded as the Platonic Ideal of Beauty. The theorems arrived at through rigorous proof are indeed absolute and eternal, but the methods used to get to them are definitely not. They represent choices that are by definition circumstantial – which is why they change as often as they do.

Petros' powerful intuition now told him that the analytic method had all but exhausted itself. The time had come for something new or, to be exact, something old, a return to the ancient, time-honoured approach to the secrets of numbers. The weighty responsibility of redefining the course of Number Theory for the future, he now decided, lay on his shoulders: a proof of Goldbach's Conjecture using the elementary, algebraic techniques would settle the matter once and for all.

As to his two first results, the Partition Theorem and the other, they could now safely be released to the general mathematical population. Since they had been arrived at through the (no longer seemingly useful to him for proving the Conjecture) analytic method, their publication could not threaten unwelcome infringements on his future research.

When he returned to Munich, his housekeeper was delighted to see the Herr Professor in such good shape. She hardly recognized him, she said, he 'looked so robust, so flushed with good health'.

It was mid-summer and, unencumbered by academic obligations, he immediately started to compose the monograph that presented his two important theorems with their proofs. Seeing once again the harvest of his ten-year hard labours with the analytic method in concrete form, with a beginning, a middle and an end, complete and presented and explained in a structured way, Petros now felt deeply satisfied. He realized that, despite the fact that he had not yet managed to prove the Conjecture, he had done excellent mathematics. It was certain that the publication of his two theorems would secure him his first significant scientific laurels. (As already mentioned, he was indifferent to the lesser, applications-oriented interest in the 'Papachristos method for the solution of differential equations'.) He could now even allow himself some gratifying daydreams of what was in store for him. He could almost see the enthusiastic letters from colleagues, the congratulations at the School, the invitations to lecture on his discoveries at all the great universities. He could even envision receiving international honours and prizes. Why not – his theorems certainly deserved them!

With the beginning of the new academic year (and still working on the monograph) Petros resumed his teaching duties. He was surprised to discover that for the first time he was now enjoying his lectures. The required effort at clarification and explanation for the sake of his students increased his own enjoyment and understanding of the material he was teaching. The Director of the School of Mathematics was obviously satisfied, not only by the improved performance he was hearing about from assistants and students alike, but mainly by the information that Professor Papachristos was preparing a monograph for publication. The two years at Innsbruck had paid off. Even though his forthcoming work apparently did not contain the proof of Goldbach's Conjecture, it was already rumoured in the School that it put forward extremely important results.

The monograph was finished a little after Christmas and it came to about two hundred pages. It was titled, with the usual slightly hypocritical modesty of many mathematicians when publishing important results, 'Some Observations on the Problem of Partitions'. Petros had it typed at the School and mailed a copy to Hardy and Littlewood, purportedly asking them to go over it lest he had slipped into an undetected pitfall, lest some less-than-obvious deductive error had escaped him. In fact, he knew well that there were no pitfalls and no errors: he just relished the thought of the two paragons of Number Theory's surprise and amazement. In fact, he was already basking in their admiration for his achievement.

After he sent off the typescript, Petros decided he owed himself a small vacation before he turned once again full-time to his work on the Conjecture. He devoted the next few days exclusively to chess.

He joined the best chess club in town, where he discovered to his delight that he could beat all but the very top players and give a hard time to the select few he could not easily overpower. He discovered a small bookshop owned by an enthusiast, where he bought weighty volumes of opening theory and collections of games. He installed the chessboard he'd bought at Innsbruck on a small table in front of his fireplace, next to a comfortable deep armchair upholstered in soft velvet. There he kept his nightly rendezvous with his new white and black friends.

This lasted for almost two weeks. 'Two *very happy* weeks,' he told me, the happiness being made greater by the anticipation of Hardy's and Littlewood's doubtless enthusiastic response to the monograph.

Yet the response, when it arrived, was anything but enthusiastic and Petros' happiness was cut short. The reaction wasn't at all what he had anticipated. In a rather short note, Hardy informed him that his first important result, the one he'd privately christened the 'Papachristos Partitions Theorem', had been discovered two years before by a young Austrian mathematician. In fact, Hardy expressed his amazement that Petros had not been aware of this, since its publication had caused a sensation in the circles of number theorists and brought great acclaim to its young author. Surely he was following the developments in the field, or wasn't he? As for his second theorem: a rather more general version of it had been proposed without proof by Ramanujan in a letter to Hardy from India, a few days before his death in 1920, one of his last great intuitions. In the years since then, the Hardy–Littlewood partnership had managed to fill in the gaps and their proof had been published in the most recent issue of the *Proceedings of the Royal Society*, of which he included a copy.

Hardy concluded his letter on a personal note, expressing his sympathy to Petros for this turn of events. With it there was the suggestion, in the understated fashion of his race and class, that it might in the future be more profitable for him to stay in closer contact with his scientific colleagues. Had Petros been living the normal life of a research mathematician, Hardy pointed out, coming to the international congresses and colloquia, corresponding with his colleagues, finding out from them the progress of their research and letting them know of his, he wouldn't have come in second in both of these otherwise extremely important discoveries. If he continued in his self-imposed isolation, another such 'unfortunate occurrence' was bound to arise.

At this point in his narrative my uncle stopped. He had been talking for several hours. It was getting dark and the birdsong in the orchard had been gradually tapering off, a solitary cricket now rhythmically piercing the silence. Uncle Petros got up and moved with tired steps to turn on a lamp, a naked bulb that cast a weak light where we were seated. As he walked back towards me, moving slowly in and out of pale yellow light and violet darkness, he looked almost like a ghost.

'So that's the explanation,' I murmured, as he sat down.

'What explanation?' he asked absently.

I told him of Sammy Epstein and his failure to find any mention of the name Petros Papachristos in the bibliographical index for Number Theory, with the exception of the early joint publications with Hardy and Littlewood on the Riemann Zeta Function. I repeated the 'burnout theory' suggested to my friend by the 'distinguished professor' at our university: that his supposed occupation with Goldbach's Conjecture had been a fabrication to disguise his inactivity.

Uncle Petros laughed bitterly.

'Oh no! It was true enough, most favoured of nephews! You can tell your friend and his "distinguished professor" that I did indeed work on trying to prove Goldbach's Conjecture – and *how* and for how *long*! Yes, and I *did* get intermediate results – wonderful, important results – but I didn't publish them when I should have done and others got in there ahead of me. Unfortunately, in mathematics there's no silver medal. The first to announce and publish gets all the glory. There's nothing left for anyone else.' He paused.

'As the saying goes, a bird in the hand is worth two in the bush and I, while pursuing the two, lost the one ...'

Somehow I didn't think the resigned serenity with which he stated this conclusion was sincere.

'But, Uncle Petros,' I asked him, 'weren't you horribly upset when you heard from Hardy?'

'Naturally I was – and "horribly" is exactly the word. I was desperate; I was overcome with anger and frustration and grief; I even briefly contemplated suicide. That was *back then*, however, another time, another self. Now, assessing my life in retrospect, I don't regret anything I did, or did not do.'

'You *don't*? You mean you don't regret the opportunity you missed to become famous, to be acknowledged as a great mathematician?'

He lifted a warning finger. 'A *very good* mathematician perhaps, but not a great one! I had discovered two good theorems, that's all.'

'That's no mean achievement, surely!'

Uncle Petros shook his head. 'Success in life is to be measured by the goals you've set yourself. There are tens of thousands of new theorems published every year the world over, but no more than a handful per century that make history!'

'Still, Uncle, you yourself say your theorems were important.'

'Look at the young man,' he countered, 'the Austrian who published *my* – as I still think of it – Partitions Theorem before me: was he raised with this result to the pedestal of a Hilbert, a Poincaré? Of course not! Perhaps he managed to secure a small niche for his portrait, somewhere in a back room of the Edifice of Mathematics . . . but if he did, so what? Or, for that matter, take Hardy and Littlewood, top-class mathematicians both of them. They possibly made the Hall of Fame – a very *large* Hall of Fame, mind you – but even they did not get their statues erected at the grand entrance alongside Euclid, Archimedes, Newton, Euler, Gauss . . . *That* had been my only ambition and nothing short of the proof of Goldbach's Conjecture, which also meant cracking the deeper mystery of the primes, could possibly have lead me there . . . .'

There was now a gleam in his eyes, a deep, focused intensity as he concluded: 'I, Petros Papachristos, never having published anything of value, will go down in mathematical history – or rather will *not* go down in it – as having achieved nothing. This suits me fine, you know. I have no regrets. Mediocrity would never have satisfied me. To an ersatz, footnote kind of immortality, I prefer my flowers, my orchard, my chessboard, the conversation I'm having with you today. Total obscurity!'

With these words, my adolescent admiration for him as Ideal Romantic Hero was rekindled. But now it was marked by large doses of realism.

'So, Uncle, it was really a question of all or nothing, eh?'

He nodded slowly. 'You could put it that way, yes.'

'And was this the end of your creative life? Did you ever again work on Goldbach's Conjecture?'

He gave me a surprised look. 'Of course I did! In fact it was after that I did my most important work.' He smiled. 'We'll come to that by and by, dear boy. Don't worry, in my story there shall be no *ignorabimus*!'

Suddenly he laughed loudly at his own joke, too loudly for comfort, I thought. Then he leaned towards me and asked me in a low voice: 'Did you learn Gödel's Incompleteness Theorem?'

'I did,' I replied, 'but I don't see what it has to do with –'

He lifted his hand roughly, cutting me short.

'"*Wir müssen wissen, wir werden wissen! In der Mathematik gibt es kein ignorabimus*",' he declaimed stridently, so loudly that his voice echoed against the pine trees and returned, to menace and haunt me. Sammy's theory of insanity instantly flashed through my mind. Could all this reminiscing have aggravated his condition? Could my uncle have finally become unhinged?

I was relieved when he continued in a more normal tone: '"We must know, we shall know! In mathematics there is no *ignorabimus*!" Thus spake the great David

Hilbert in the International Congress, in 1900. A proclamation of mathematics as the heaven of Absolute Truth. The vision of Euclid, the vision of Consistency and Completeness...'

Uncle Petros resumed his story.

The vision of Euclid had been the transformation of a random collection of numerical and geometric observations into a well-articulated system, where one can proceed from the *a priori* accepted elementary truths and advance, applying logical operations, step by step, to rigorous proof of all true statements: mathematics as a tree with strong roots (the Axioms), a solid trunk (Rigorous Proof) and ever growing branches blooming with wondrous flowers (the Theorems). All later mathematicians, geometers, number theorists, algebraists, and more recently analysts, topologists, algebraic geometers, group-theorists, etc., the practitioners of all the new disciplines that keep emerging to this day (new branches of the same ancient tree) never veered from the great pioneer's course: Axioms–Rigorous Proof–Theorems.

With a bitter smile, Petros remembered the constant exhortation of Hardy to anyone (especially poor Ramanujan, whose mind produced them like grass on fertile soil) bothering him with hypotheses: 'Prove it! Prove it!' Indeed, Hardy liked saying, if a heraldic motto were needed for a noble family of mathematicians, there could be no better than *Quod Erat Demonstrandum*.

In 1900, during the Second International Congress of Mathematicians, held in Paris, Hilbert announced that the time had come to extend the ancient dream to its ultimate consequences. Mathematicians now had at their disposal, as Euclid had not, the language of Formal Logic, which allowed them to examine, in a rigorous way, mathematics itself. The holy trinity of Axioms–Rigorous Proof–Theorems should hence be applied not only to the numbers, shapes or algebraic identities of the various mathematical theories but to the very theories themselves. Mathematicians could at last rigorously demonstrate what for two millennia had been their central, unquestioned credo, the core of the vision: that in mathematics every true statement is provable.

A few years later, Russell and Whitehead published their monumental *Principia Mathematica*, proposing for the first time a totally precise way of speaking about deduction, Proof Theory. Yet although this new tool brought with it great promise of a final answer to Hilbert's demand, the two English logicians fell short of actually demonstrating the critical property. The 'completeness of mathematical theories' (i.e. the fact that within them every true statement is provable) had not yet been proven, but there was now not the smallest doubt in anybody's mind or heart that one day, very soon, it would be. Mathematicians continued to believe, as Euclid had believed, that they dwelt in the Realm of Absolute Truth. The victorious cry emerging from the Paris Congress, 'We *must* know, we *shall* know, in Mathematics there is no *ignorabimus,*' still constituted the one unshakable article of faith of every working mathematician.

I interrupted this rather exalted historical excursion: 'I know all this, Uncle. Once you enjoined me to learn Gödel's theorem I obviously also had to find out about its background.'

'It's not the background,' he corrected me; 'it's the psychology. You have to understand the emotional climate in which mathematicians worked in those happy days, before Kurt Gödel. You asked me how I mustered up the courage to continue after my great disappointment. Well, here's how . . . .'

Despite the fact that he hadn't yet managed to attain his goal and prove Goldbach's Conjecture, Uncle Petros firmly believed that his goal was attainable. Being himself Euclid's spiritual great-grandson, his trust in this was complete. Since the Conjecture was almost certainly valid (nobody with the exception of Ramanujan and his vague 'hunch' had ever seriously doubted this), the proof of it existed somewhere, in some form.

He continued with an example:

'Suppose a friend states that he has mislaid a key somewhere in his house and asks you to help him find it. If you believe his memory to be faultless and you have absolute trust in his integrity, what does it mean?'

'It means that he has indeed mislaid the key somewhere in his house.'

'And if he further ascertains that no one else entered the house since?'

'Then we can assume that it was not taken out of the house.'

'*Ergo*?'

'*Ergo*, the key is still there, and if we search long enough – the house being finite – sooner or later we will find it.'

My uncle applauded. 'Excellent! It is precisely this certainty that fuelled my optimism anew. After I had recovered from my first disappointment I got up one fine morning and said to myself: "What the hell – that proof is still out there, somewhere!"'

'And so?'

'And so, my boy, since the proof existed, one had but to find it!'

I wasn't following his reasoning.

'I don't see how this provided comfort, Uncle Petros: the fact that proof existed didn't in any way imply that *you* would be the one to discover it!'

He glared at me for not immediately seeing the obvious. 'Was there anyone in the whole wide world better equipped to do so than I, Petros Papachristos?' The question was obviously rhetorical and so I didn't bother to answer it. But I was puzzled: the Petros Papachristos he was referring to was a different man from the self-effacing, withdrawn senior citizen I'd known since childhood.

Of course, it had taken him some time to recover from reading Hardy's letter and its disheartening news. Yet recover he eventually did. He pulled himself together and, his deposits of hope refilled through the belief in 'the existence of the proof somewhere out there', he resumed his quest, a slightly changed man. His misadventure, by exposing an element of vanity in his manic search, had created in him an inner core of peace, a sense of life continuing irrespective of Goldbach's Conjecture. His working schedule now became slightly more relaxed, his mind also aided by interludes of chess, more tranquil despite the constant effort.

In addition, the switch to the algebraic method, already decided in Innsbruck, made him feel once again the excitement of a fresh start, the exhilaration of entering virgin territory.

For a hundred years, from Riemann's paper in the mid-nineteenth century, the dominant trend in Number Theory had been analytic. By now resorting to the ancient, elementary approach, my uncle was in the vanguard of an important regression, if I may be allowed the oxymoron. The historians of mathematics will do well to remember him for this, if for no other part of his work.

It must be stressed here that, in the context of Number Theory, the word 'elementary' can on no account be considered synonymous with 'simple' and even less so with 'easy'. Its techniques are those of Diophantus', Euclid's, Fermat's, Gauss's and Euler's great results and are elementary only in the sense of deriving from the elements of mathematics, the basic arithmetical operations and the methods of classical algebra on the real numbers. Despite the effectiveness of the analytic techniques, the elementary method stays closer to the fundamental properties of the integers and the results arrived at with it are, in an intuitive way clear to the mathematician, more profound.

Gossip had by now seeped out from Cambridge, that Petros Papachristos of Munich University had had a bit of bad luck, deferring publication of very important work. Fellow number theorists began to seek his opinions. He was invited to their meetings, which from that point on he would invariably attend, enlivening his monotonous lifestyle with occasional travel. The news had also leaked out (thanks here to the Director of the School of Mathematics) that he was working on the notoriously difficult Conjecture of Goldbach, and that made his colleagues look on him with a mixture of awe and sympathy.

At an international meeting, about a year after his return to Munich, he ran across Littlewood. 'How's the work going on Goldbach, old chap?' he asked Petros.

'Always at it.'

'Is it true what I hear, that you're using algebraic methods?'

'It's true.'

Littlewood expressed his doubts and Petros surprised himself by talking freely about the content of his research. 'After all, Littlewood,' he concluded, 'I know the problem better than anyone else. My intuition tells me the truth expressed by the Conjecture is so fundamental that only an elementary approach can reveal it.'

Littlewood shrugged. 'I respect your intuition, Papachristos; it's just that you are totally isolated. Without a constant exchange of ideas, you may find yourself grappling with phantoms before you know it.'

'So what do you recommend,' Petros joked, 'issuing weekly reports of the progress of my research?'

'Listen,' said Littlewood seriously, 'you should find a few people whose judgement and integrity you trust. Start sharing; exchange, old chap!'

The more he thought about this suggestion, the more it made sense. Much to his surprise he realized that, far from frightening him, the prospect of discussing the progress of his work now filled him with pleasurable anticipation. Of course his audience would have to be small, very small indeed. If it was to consist of people 'whose judgement and integrity he trusted', that would of necessity mean an audience of no more than two: Hardy and Littlewood.

He started anew the correspondence with them that he'd interrupted a couple of years after he left Cambridge. Without stating it in so many words, he dropped hints about his intention to bring about a meeting during which he would present his work. Around Christmas of 1931, he received an official invitation to spend the next year at Trinity College. He knew that since, for all practical purposes, he had been absent from the mathematical world for a long long time, Hardy must have used all his influence to secure the offer. Gratitude, combined with the exciting prospect of a creative exchange with the two great number theorists, made him immediately accept.

Petros described his first few months in England, in the academic year 1932–33, as probably the happiest of his life. Memories of his first stay there, fifteen years earlier, infused his days at Cambridge with the enthusiasm of early youth, as yet untainted by the possibility of failure.

Soon after he arrived, he presented to Hardy and Littlewood the outline of his work to date with the algebraic method, and this gave him the first taste, after more than a decade, of the joy of peer recognition. It took him several mornings, standing at the blackboard in Hardy's office, to trace his progress in the three years since his volte-face from the analytic techniques. His two renowned colleagues, who were at first extremely sceptical, now began to see some advantages to his approach, Littlewood more so than Hardy.

'You must realize,' the latter told him, 'that you're running a huge risk. If you don't manage to ride this approach to the end, you'll be left with precious little to show for it. Intermediate divisibility results, although quite charming, are not of much interest any more. Unless you can convince people that they can be useful in proving important theorems, like the Conjecture, they are not of themselves worth much.'

Petros was, as always, well aware of the risks he was taking.

'Still, something tells me you may well be on a good course,' Littlewood encouraged him.

'Yes,' grumbled Hardy, 'but please do hurry up, Papachristos, before your mind begins to rot, the way mine's doing. Remember, at your age Ramanujan was already five years dead!'

This first presentation had taken place early in the Michaelmas term, yellow leaves falling outside the Gothic windows. During the winter months that followed, my uncle's work advanced more than it ever had. It was at this time that he also started using the method he called 'geometric'.

He began by representing all composite (i.e. non-prime) numbers by placing dots in a parallelogram, with the lowest prime divisor as width and the quotient of the number by it as height. For example, 15 is represented by 3 × 5 rows, 25 by 5 × 5, 35 by 5 × 7 rows:

By this method, all even numbers are represented as double columns, as 2 × 2, 2 × 3, 2 × 4, 2 × 5, etc.

The primes, on the contrary, since they have no integer divisors, are represented as single rows, for example 5, 7, 11:

• • • • •　　• • • • • • •　　　• • • • • • • • • •

Petros extended the insights from this elementary geometric analogy to arrive at number-theoretical conclusions.

After Christmas, he presented his first results. Since, however, instead of using pen and paper, he laid out his patterns on the floor of Hardy's study using beans, his new approach earned from Littlewood a teasing accolade. Although the younger man conceded that he found 'the famous Papachristos bean method' conceivably of some usefulness, Hardy was by now outright annoyed.

'Beans indeed!' he said. 'There is a world of difference between elementary and infantile . . . Don't you forget it, Papachristos, this blasted Conjecture is *difficult* – if it weren't, Goldbach would have proved it himself!'

Petros, however, had faith in his intuition and attributed Hardy's reaction to the 'intellectual constipation brought about by age' (his words).

'The great truths in life are simple,' he told Littlewood later, when the two of them were having tea in his rooms. Littlewood countered him, mentioning the extremely complex proof of the Prime Number Theorem by Hadamard and de la Vallée-Poussin.

Then he made a proposal: 'What would you say to doing some *real* mathematics, old chap? I've been working for some time now on Hilbert's Tenth Problem, the solvability of Diophantine equations. I have this idea that I want to test, but I'm afraid I need help with the algebra. Do you think you could lend me a hand?'

Littlewood would have to seek his algebraic help elsewhere, however. Although his colleague's confidence in him was a boost to Petros' pride, he flatly declined. He was too exclusively involved with the Conjecture, he said, too deeply engrossed in it, to be able fruitfully to concern himself with anything else.

His faith, backed by a stubborn intuition, in the 'infantile' (according to Hardy) geometric approach, was such that for the first time since he began work on the Conjecture, Petros now often had the feeling that he was almost a hair's breadth away from the proof. There were actually even a few exhilarating minutes, late on a sunny January afternoon, when he had the short-lived illusion that he had succeeded – but, alas, a more sober examination located a small, but crucial mistake.

(I have to confess it, dear reader: at this point in my uncle's narrative I felt despite myself a quiver of vengeful joy. I remembered that summer in Pylos, a few years back, when I too had thought for a while I'd discovered the proof of Goldbach's Conjecture – although I did not then know it by name.)

His great optimism notwithstanding, Petros' occasional bouts of self-doubt, sometimes verging on despair (especially after Hardy's put-down of the geometric method), now became stronger than ever. Still, they could not curb his spirit. He fought them away by branding them the inevitable anguish preceding a great triumph, the onset of the labour pains leading into the delivery of the majestic discovery. After all, the night is darkest before dawn. He was, Petros felt certain, all but ready to run the final dash. One last concentrated burst of effort was all that was needed to award him the last brilliant insight.

Then, there would come the glorious finish . . .

The heralding of Petros Papachristos' surrender, the termination of his efforts to prove Goldbach's Conjecture, came in a dream he had in Cambridge, sometime after Christmas – a portent whose full significance he did not at first fathom.

Like many mathematicians working for long periods with basic arithmetical problems, Petros had acquired the quality that has been called 'friendship with the integers', an extended knowledge of the idiosyncrasy, quirks and peculiarities of thousands of specific whole numbers. A few examples: a 'friend of the integers' will immediately recognize 199 or 457 or 1009 as primes. 220 he will automatically associate with 284 since they are linked by an unusual relationship (the sum of the integer divisors of each one is equal to the other). 256 he reads naturally as 2 to the eighth power, which he well knows to be followed by a number with great historical interest, since 257 can be expressed as $2^{2^2}+1$, and a famous hypothesis held that all numbers of the form $2^{2^n} + 1$ were prime.[*]

The first man my uncle had met who had this quality (and to the utmost degree) was Srinivasa Ramanujan. Petros had seen it demonstrated on many opportunities, and to me he recounted this anecdote:[†]

One day in 1918, he and Hardy were visiting him in the sanatorium where he lay ill. To break the ice, Hardy mentioned that the taxi that had brought them had had the registration number 1729, which he personally found 'rather boring'. But Ramanujan, after

[*] It was Fermat who first stated the general form, obviously generalizing from age-old observations that this was true of the first four values of n, i.e. $2^{2^1} + 1 = 5$, $2^{2^2} + 1 = 17$, $2^{2^3} + 1 = 257$, $2^{2^4} + 1 = 65{,}537$, all prime. However, it was later shown that for $n = 5$, $2^{2^5} + 1$ equals $4{,}294{,}967{,}297$, a number which is composite, since it's divisible by the primes 641 and 6,700,417. Conjectures are not always proved correct!
[†] Hardy also recounts the incident in his *Mathematician's Apology* without, however, acknowledging my uncle's presence.

pondering this for only a moment, disagreed vehemently: 'No, no, Hardy! It's a particularly interesting number – in fact, it's the smallest integer that can be expressed as the sum of two cubes in two different ways!'*

During the years that Petros worked on the Conjecture with the elementary approach, his own friendship with the integers developed to an extraordinary degree. Numbers ceased after a while being inanimate entities; they became to him almost alive, each with a distinct personality. In fact, together with the certainty that the solution existed somewhere out there, it added to his resolve to persevere during the most difficult of times: working with the integers, he felt, to quote him directly, 'constantly among friends'.

This familiarity caused an influx of specific numbers into his dreams. Out of the nameless, nondescript mass of integers that up until then crowded their nightly dramas, individual actors now began to emerge, even occasional protagonists. 65, for example, appeared for some reason as a City gentleman, with bowler hat and rolled umbrella, in constant companionship with one of his prime divisors, 13, a goblin-like creature, supple and lightning-quick. 333 was a fat slob, stealing bites of food from the mouths of its sib-

---

* Indeed, $1729 = 12^3 + 1^3 = 10^3 + 9^3$, a property which does not apply for any smaller integer.

lings 222 and 111, and 8191, a number known as a 'Mersenne Prime', invariably wore the attire of a French *gamin*, complete down to the Gauloise cigarette hanging from his lips.

Some of the visions were amusing and pleasant, others indifferent, still others repetitious and annoying. There was one category of arithmetical dream, however, which could only be called nightmarish, if not for horror or agony then for its profound, bottomless sadness. Particular even numbers would appear, personified as pairs of identical twins. (Remember that an even number is always of the form $2k$, the sum of two equal integers). The twins would gaze on him fixedly, immobile and expressionless. But there was great, if mute, anguish in their eyes, the anguish of desperation. If they could have spoken, their words would have been: 'Come! Please. Hurry! Set us free!'

It was a variation on these sad apparitions that came to wake him one night late in January 1933. This was the dream that he termed in retrospect 'the herald of defeat'.

He dreamed of 2^{100} (2 to the hundredth power, an enormous number) personified as two identical, freckled, beautiful dark-eyed girls, looking straight into his eyes. But now there wasn't just sadness in their look, as there had been in his previous visions of the Evens; there was anger, hatred even. After gazing at him for a long, long while (this in itself was sufficient cause to brand the dream a nightmare) one of the twins suddenly shook her head from side to side with jerky, abrupt movements. Then her mouth was contorted into a cruel smile, the cruelty being that of a rejected lover.

'You'll never get us,' she hissed.

At this, Petros, drenched in sweat, jumped up from his bed. The words that 2^{99} (that's one half of 2^{100}) had spoken meant only one thing: He was not fated to prove the Conjecture. Of course, he was not a superstitious old woman who would give undue credence to omens. Yet the profound exhaustion of many fruitless years had now begun to take its toll. His nerves were not as strong as they used to be and the dream upset him inordinately.

Unable to go back to sleep, he went out to walk in the dark, foggy streets, to try to shake off its dreary feeling. As he walked in the first light among the ancient stone buildings, he suddenly heard fast footsteps approaching behind him, and for a moment he was seized by panic and turned sharply round. A young man in athletic gear materialized out of the mist, running energetically, uttered a greeting and disappeared once again, his rhythmic breathing trailing off into complete silence.

Still upset by the nightmare, Petros wasn't sure

whether this image had been real, or an overflow of his dream world. When, however, a few months later the very same young man came to his rooms at Trinity on a fateful mission, he instantly recognized him as the early-morning runner. After he was gone, he realized with hindsight that their first, dawn meeting had cryptically signalled the dark forewarning, coming as it did after the vision of 2^{100}, with its message of defeat.

The fatal meeting took place a few months after the first, early-morning encounter. In his diary Petros marks the exact date with a laconic comment – the first and last use of Christian reference I discovered in his diaries: '17 March 1933. Kurt Gödel's Theorem. May Mary, Mother of God, have mercy on me!'

It was late afternoon and he had been in his rooms all day, sitting forward in his armchair studying parallelograms of beans laid out on the floor before him, lost in thought, when there was a knock on the door.

'Professor Papachristos?'

A blond head appeared. Petros had a powerful visual memory and immediately recognized the young runner, who was full of excuses for disturbing him. 'Please forgive my barging in on you like this, Professor,' he said, 'but I am desperate for your help.'

Petros was quite surprised – he'd thought his presence at Cambridge had gone completely unremarked.

He wasn't famous, he wasn't even well known and, except at his almost nightly appearances at the university chess club, he hadn't exchanged two words with anyone other than Hardy and Littlewood during his stay.

'My help on what subject?'

'Oh, in deciphering a difficult German text – a *mathematical* text.' The young man apologized again for presuming to take up his time with such a lowly task. This particular article, however, was of such great importance to him that when he heard that a senior mathematician from Germany was at Trinity, he couldn't resist appealing to him for assistance in its precise translation.

There was something so childishly eager in his manner that Petros couldn't refuse him.

'I'd be glad to help you, if I can. What field is the article in?'

'Formal Logic, Professor. The *Grundlagen*, the Foundations of Mathematics.'

Petros felt a rush of relief that it wasn't in Number Theory – he'd feared for a moment the young caller might have wanted to pump him on his work on the Conjecture, using help with the language merely as an excuse. As he was more or less finished with his day's work, he asked the young visitor to take a seat.

'What did you say your name was?'

'It's Alan Turing, Professor. I'm an undergraduate.'

Turing handed him the journal containing the article, opened at the right page.

'Ah, the *Monatshefte für Mathematik und Physik*,' said Petros, 'the *Monthly Review for Mathematics and Physics*, a highly esteemed publication. The title of the article is, I see, "Über formal unentscheidbare Sätze der *Principia Mathematica* und verwandter Systeme". In translation this would be . . . Let's see . . . "On the formally undecidable propositions of *Principia Mathematica* and similar systems". The author is a Mr Kurt Gödel, from Vienna. Is he well known in this field?'

Turing looked at him surprised. 'You don't mean to say you haven't heard of this article, Professor?'

Petros smiled: 'My dear young man, mathematics too has been infected by the modern plague, overspecialization. I'm afraid I have no idea of what's being accomplished in Formal Logic, or any other field for that matter. Outside of Number Theory I am, alas, a complete innocent.'

'But Professor,' Turing protested, 'Gödel's Theorem is of interest to *all* mathematicians, and number theorists especially! Its first application is to the very basis of arithmetic, the Peano–Dedekind axiomatic system.'

To Turing's amazement, Petros also wasn't too clear about the Peano–Dedekind axiomatic system. Like most working mathematicians he considered Formal

Logic, the field whose main subject is mathematics itself, a preoccupation that was certainly over-fussy and quite possibly altogether unnecessary. Its tireless attempts at rigorous foundation and its endless examination of basic principles he regarded, more or less, as a waste of time. The piece of popular wisdom, 'If it ain't broke, don't fix it,' could well define this attitude: a mathematician's job was to try to prove theorems, not perpetually ponder the status of their unspoken and unquestioned basis.

In spite of this, however, the passion with which his young visitor spoke had aroused Petros' curiosity. 'So, what did this young Mr Gödel prove, that is of such interest to number theorists?'

'He solved the Problem of Completeness,' Turing announced with stars in his eyes.

Petros smiled. The Problem of Completeness was nothing other than the quest for a formal demonstration of the fact that all true statements are ultimately provable.

'Oh, good,' Petros said politely. 'I have to tell you, however – no offence meant to Mr Gödel, of course – that to the active researcher, the completeness of mathematics has always been obvious. Still, it's nice to know that someone finally sat down and proved it.'

But Turing was vehemently shaking his head, his face flushed with excitement. 'That's exactly the point,

Professor Papachristos: Gödel *did not* prove it!'

Petros was puzzled. 'I don't understand, Mr Turing ... You just said this young man solved the Problem of Completeness, didn't you?'

'Yes, Professor, but contrary to everybody's expectation – Hilbert's and Russell's included – he solved it in the negative! He proved that arithmetic and all mathematical theories are *not* complete!'

Petros was not familiar enough with the concepts of Formal Logic immediately to realize the full implications of these words. 'I beg your pardon?'

Turing knelt by his armchair, his finger stabbing excitedly at the arcane symbols filling Gödel's article. 'Here: this genius proved – *conclusively proved!* – that no matter what axioms you accept, a theory of numbers will of necessity contain unprovable propositions!'

'You mean, of course, the *false* propositions?'

'No, I mean *true* propositions – true yet impossible to prove!'

Petros jumped to his feet. 'This is not possible!'

'Oh yes it is, and the proof of it is right here, in these fifteen pages: "Truth is not always provable!"'

My uncle now felt a sudden dizziness overcome him. 'But ... but this cannot be.'

He flipped hurriedly through the pages, striving to absorb in a single moment, if possible, the article's intricate argument, mumbling on, indifferent to the young man's presence.

'It is obscene . . . an abnormality . . . an aberration . . .'

Turing was smiling smugly. 'That's how all mathematicians react at first . . . But Russell and Whitehead have examined Gödel's proof and proclaimed it to be flawless. In fact, the term they used was "exquisite".'

Petros grimaced. '"Exquisite"? But what it proves – if it really proves it, which I refuse to believe – is the *end of mathematics*!'

For hours he pored over the brief but extremely dense text. He translated as Turing explained to him the underlying concepts of Formal Logic, with which he was unfamiliar. When they'd finished they took it again from the top, going over the proof step by step, Petros desperately seeking a faulty step in the deduction.

This was the beginning of the end.

It was past midnight when Turing left. Petros couldn't sleep. First thing the next morning he went to see Littlewood. To his great surprise, he already knew of Gödel's Incompleteness Theorem.

'How could you not have mentioned it even once?' Petros asked him. 'How could you know of the existence of something like that and be so calm about it?'

Littlewood didn't understand: 'What are you so upset about, old chap? Gödel is researching some very special cases; he's looking into paradoxes apparently inherent in all axiomatic systems. What does this have to do with us line-of-combat mathematicians?'

However, Petros was not so easily appeased. 'But, don't you see, Littlewood? From now on, we have to ask of every statement still unproved whether it can be a case of application of the Incompleteness Theorem . . . Every outstanding hypothesis or conjecture can be *a priori* undemonstrable! Hilbert's "in mathematics there is no *ignorabimus*" no longer applies; the very ground that we stood on has been pulled out from under our feet!'

Littlewood shrugged. 'I don't see the point of getting all worked up about the few unprovable truths, when there are billions of provable ones to tackle!'

'Yes, damn it, but how do we know *which is which*?'

Although Littlewood's calm reaction should have been comforting, a welcome note of optimism after the previous evening's disaster, it didn't provide Petros with a definite answer to the one and only, dizzying, terrifying question that had jumped into his mind the moment he'd heard of Gödel's result. The question was so horrible he hardly dared formulate it: what if the Incompleteness Theorem also applied to *his* problem? What if Goldbach's Conjecture was unprovable?

From Littlewood's rooms he went straight to Alan Turing, at his college, and asked him whether there had been any further progress in the matter of the Incompleteness Theorem, after Gödel's original paper. Turing didn't know. Apparently, there was only one person in the world who could answer his question.

Petros left a note to Hardy and Littlewood saying he had some urgent business in Munich and crossed the Channel that same evening. The next day he was in Vienna. He tracked his man down through an academic acquaintance. They spoke on the telephone and, since Petros didn't want to be seen at the university, they made an appointment to meet at the café of the Sacher Hotel.

Kurt Gödel arrived precisely on time, a thin young man of average height, with small myopic eyes behind thick glasses.

Petros didn't waste any time: 'There is something I want to ask you, Herr Gödel, in strict confidentiality.'

Gödel, by nature uncomfortable at social intercourse, was now even more so. 'Is this a personal matter, Herr Professor?'

'It is professional, but as it refers to my personal research I would appreciate it – indeed, I would demand! – that it remain strictly between you and me. Please let me know, Herr Gödel: is there a procedure for determining whether your theorem applies to a given hypothesis?'

Gödel gave him the answer he'd feared. 'No.'

'So you cannot, in fact, *a priori* determine which statements are provable and which are not?'

'As far as I know, Professor, every unproved statement can in principle be unprovable.'

At this, Petros saw red. He felt the irresistible urge to grab the father of the Incompleteness Theorem by the scruff of the neck and bang his head on the shining surface of the table. However, he restrained himself, leaned forward and clasped his arm tightly.

'I've spent my whole life trying to prove Goldbach's Conjecture,' he told him in a low, intense voice, 'and now you're telling me it may be unprovable?'

Gödel's already pale face was now totally drained of colour.

'In theory, yes –'

'Damn theory, man!' Petros' shout made the heads of the Sacher café's distinguished clientèle turn in their direction. 'I need to *be certain*, don't you understand? I have a right to know whether I'm wasting my life!'

He was squeezing his arm so hard that Gödel grimaced in pain. Suddenly, Petros felt shame at the way he was carrying on. After all, the poor man wasn't personally responsible for the incompleteness of mathematics – all he had done was discover it! He released his arm, mumbling apologies.

Gödel was shaking. 'I un-understand how you fe-

feel, Professor,' he stammered, 'but I-I'm afraid that for the time being there is no way to answer yo-your question.'

From then on, the vague threat hinted at by Gödel's Incompleteness Theorem developed into a relentless anxiety that gradually came to shadow his every living moment and finally quench his fighting spirit.

This didn't happen overnight, of course. Petros persisted in his research for a few more years, but he was now a changed man. From that point on, when he worked he worked half-heartedly, but when he despaired his despair was total, so insufferable in fact that it took on the form of indifference, a much more bearable feeling.

'You see,' Petros explained to me, 'from the first moment I heard of it, the Incompleteness Theorem destroyed the certainty that had fuelled my efforts. It told me there was a definite probability I had been wandering inside a labyrinth whose exit I'd never find, even if I had a hundred lifetimes to give to the search. And this for a very simple reason: because it was possible that the exit didn't exist, that the labyrinth was an infinity of cul-de-sacs! O, most favoured of nephews, I began to believe that I had wasted my life chasing a chimera!'

He illustrated his new situation by resorting once

again to the example he'd given me earlier. The hypo-thetical friend who had enlisted his help in seeking a key mislaid in his house might (or again might not, *but there was no way to know which*) be suffering from amne-sia. It was possible that the 'lost key' had never existed in the first place!

The comforting reassurance, on which his efforts of two decades had rested, had, from one moment to the next, ceased to apply, and frequent visitations of the Even Numbers increased his anxiety. Practically every night now they would return, injecting his dreams with evil portent. New images haunted his nightmares, constant variations on themes of failure and defeat. High walls were being erected between him and the Even Numbers, which were retreating in droves, farther and farther away, heads lowered, a sad, vanquished army receding into the darkness of desolate, wide, empty spaces . . . Yet, the worst of these visions, the one that never failed to wake him trembling and drenched in sweat, was of 2^{100}, the two freckled, dark-eyed, beautiful girls. They gazed at him mutely, their eyes brimming with tears, then slowly turned their heads away, again and again, their features being gradually consumed by dark-ness.

The dream's meaning was clear; its bleak symbol-ism did not need a soothsayer or a psychoanalyst to decipher it: alas, the Incompleteness Theorem applied to his problem. Goldbach's Conjecture was *a priori* unprovable.

Upon his return to Munich after the year in Cambridge, Petros resumed the external routine he had established before his departure: teaching, chess, and also a minimum of social life; since he now had nothing better to do, he began to accept the occasional invitation. It was the first time since his earliest childhood that preoccupation with mathematical truths didn't occupy the central role in his life. And although he did continue his research awhile, the old fervour was gone. From then on he spent no more than a few hours a day at it, working half-absently at his geometric method. He'd still wake up before dawn, go to his study and pace slowly up and down, picking his way among the parallelograms of beans laid out on the floor (he had pushed all the furniture against the walls to make room). He picked up a few here, added a few there, muttering absently to himself. This went on for a while and then, sooner or later, he drifted towards the armchair, sat, sighed and turned his attention to the chessboard.

This routine went on for another two or three years, the time spent daily at this erratic form of 'research' continuously decreasing to almost nil. Then, near the end of 1936, Petros received a telegram from Alan Turing, who was now at Princeton University:

I HAVE PROVED THE IMPOSSIBILITY OF A PRIORI DECIDABILITY STOP.

Exactly: STOP. This meant, in effect, that it was impossible to know in advance whether a particular mathematical statement is provable: if it is eventually proven, then it obviously is – what Turing had managed to show was that as long as it remains *un*proven, there is absolutely no way of ascertaining whether its proof is impossible or simply very difficult.

The immediate corollary of this, which concerned Petros, was that if he chose to pursue the proof of Goldbach's Conjecture, he would be doing so at his own risk. If he continued with his research, it would have to be out of sheer optimism and positive fighting spirit. Of these two qualities, however – time, exhaustion, ill luck, Kurt Gödel and now Alan Turing assisting – he had run out.

STOP.

A few days after Turing's telegram (the date he gives in his diary is 7 December 1936) Petros informed his housekeeper that the beans would no longer be required. She swept them all up, gave them a good wash and turned them into a hearty *cassoulet* for the Herr Professor's dinner.

*

Uncle Petros remained silent for a while, looking dejectedly at his hands. Beyond the small circle of pale yellow light around us, cast by the single light-bulb, there was now total darkness.

'So that's when you gave up?' I asked softly.

He nodded. 'Yes.'

'And you never again worked on Goldbach's Conjecture?'

'Never.'

'What about Isolde?'

My question seemed to startle him. 'Isolde? What about her?'

'I thought that it was to win her love you decided to prove the Conjecture – no?'

Uncle Petros smiled sadly.

'Isolde gave me "the beautiful journey", as our poet says. Without her I might "never have set out".* Yet, she was no more than the original stimulus. A few years after I had begun my work on the Conjecture her memory faded, she became no more than a phantasm, a bittersweet recollection . . . My ambitions became of a higher, more exalted variety.'

He sighed. 'Poor Isolde! She was killed during the Allied bombardment of Dresden, along with her two

---

* C. Cavafy, 'Ithaca'.

daughters. Her husband, the "dashing young lieutenant" for whom she'd abandoned me, had died earlier on the Eastern Front.'

The last part of my uncle's story had no particular
mathematical interest:

In the years that followed history, not mathematics,
became the determining force in his life. World events
broke down the protective barrier which till then had
kept him safe within the ivory tower of his research. In
1938, the Gestapo arrested his housekeeper and sent
her to what was still in those days referred to as a 'work
camp'. He didn't hire anybody to take her place,
naïvely believing that she'd return soon, her arrest due
to some 'misunderstanding'. (After the war's end he
learned from a surviving relative that she'd died in
1943 in Dachau, just a short distance from Munich.) He
started to eat out, returning home only to sleep. When
he was not at the university he would hang out at the
chess club, playing, watching or analysing games.

In 1939, the Director of the School of Mathematics,
by then a prominent member of the Nazi party, indicated that Petros should immediately apply for German citizenship and formally become a subject of the
Third Reich. He refused, not for any reasons of principle (Petros managed to go through life unhampered
by any ideological burden) but because the last thing

he wanted was to be involved once again with differential equations. Apparently, it was the Ministry of Defence that had suggested he apply for citizenship, with precisely this aim in mind. After his refusal he became in essence a *persona non grata*. In September 1940, a little before Italy's declaration of war on Greece would have made him an enemy alien subject to internment, he was fired from his post. After a friendly warning, he left Germany.

Having, by the strict criterion of published work, been mathematically inactive for more than twenty years, Petros was now academically unemployable and so he had to return to his homeland. During the first years of the country's occupation by the Axis powers he lived in the family house in central Athens, on Queen Sophia Avenue, with his recently widowed father and his newly-wed brother Anargyros (my parents had moved to their own house), devoting practically all his time to chess. Very soon, however, my newborn cousins with their cries and toddler activities became a much greater annoyance to him than the occupying Fascists and Nazis and he moved to the small, rarely used family cottage in Ekali.

After the Liberation, my grandfather managed to secure for Petros the offer of the Chair of Analysis at Athens University, through string-pulling and manoeuvring. He turned it down, however, using the spurious excuse that 'it would interfere with his research'. (In this instance, my friend Sammy's theory of Goldbach's Conjecture as my uncle's pretext for idleness proved completely correct.) Two years later, paterfamilias Papachristos died, leaving to his three sons equal shares of his business and the principal executive positions exclusively to my father and Anargyros. 'My eldest, Petros,' his will expressly decreed, 'shall retain the privilege of pursuing his important mathematical research,' i.e. the privilege of being supported by his brothers without doing any work.

'And after that?' I asked, still cherishing the hope that a surprise might be in store, an unexpected reversal on the last page.

'After that nothing,' my uncle concluded. 'For almost twenty years my life has been as you know it: chess and gardening, gardening and chess. Oh, and once a month a visit to the philanthropic institution founded by your grandfather, to help them with the book-keeping. It's something towards the salvation of my soul, just in case there exists a hereafter.'

It was midnight by this time and I was exhausted. Still, I thought I should end the evening on a positive note and, after a big yawn and a stretch, I said: 'You are admirable, Uncle . . . if not for anything else, for the courage and magnanimity with which you accepted failure.'

This comment, however, got a reaction of utter surprise. 'What are you talking about?' my uncle said. 'I didn't fail!'

Now the surprise was mine. 'You didn't?'

'Oh no, no, no, dear boy!' He shook his head from side to side. 'I see you didn't understand anything. I didn't fail – I was just unlucky!'

'*Unlucky?* You mean unlucky to have chosen such a difficult problem?'

'No,' he said, now looking totally amazed at my inability to grasp an obvious point. 'Unlucky – that, by the way, is a mild word for it – to have chosen a problem that had no solution. Weren't you listening?' He sighed heavily. 'By and by, my suspicions were confirmed: Goldbach's Conjecture is unprovable!'

'But how can you be so sure about it?' I asked.

'Intuition,' he answered with a shrug. 'It is the only tool left to the mathematician in the absence of proof. For a truth to be so fundamental, so simple to state, and yet so unimaginably resistant to any form of systematic reasoning, there could have been no other explanation. Unbeknown to me I had undertaken a Sisyphean task.'

I frowned. 'I don't know about that,' I said. 'But the way I see it –'

Now, however, Uncle Petros interrupted me with a laugh. 'You may be a bright boy,' he said, 'but math-

ematically you are still no more than a foetus – whereas
I, in my time, was a veritable, full-blown giant. So, don't
go weighing your intuition against mine, most favoured
of nephews!'

Against that, of course, I couldn't argue.

Three

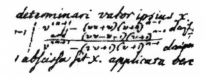

My first reaction to this extensive autobiographical account was one of admiration. Uncle Petros had given me the facts of his life with remarkable honesty. It wasn't until a few days later, when the oppressive influence of his melancholy narrative diminished, that I realized everything he'd told me had been beside the point.

Remember that our meeting had been initially arranged so that he could try to justify himself. His life's story was only relevant to the extent that it explained his atrocious behaviour, assigning me in all my adolescent mathematical innocence the task of proving Goldbach's Conjecture. Yet, during his long narrative he had not even touched on his cruel prank. He'd ranted on and on about his own failure (or maybe I should do him the favour of calling it 'bad luck'), but about his decision to turn *me* away from studying mathematics and the method he had chosen to implement it, not a single word. Did he expect me automatically to draw the conclusion that his behaviour to me was determined by his own bitter life-experiences? It didn't follow: although his life story was indeed a valid cautionary tale, it taught a future mathematician what pitfalls to avoid so as to make the most of his career – not how to terminate it.

I let a few days go by before I went back to Ekali and asked him point-blank: could he now explain why he had attempted to dissuade me from following my inclination.

Uncle Petros shrugged. 'Do you want the truth?'

'Of course, Uncle.' I said. 'What else?'

'All right then. I believed from the first moment – and still do, I'm sorry to say – that you have no special gift for great mathematics.'

I became, once again, furious. 'Oh? And how on earth could you have known that? Did you ask me a single mathematical question? Did you ever set me a problem to solve, other than the unprovable, as you termed it, Conjecture of Christian Goldbach? I certainly hope you don't have the nerve to tell me that you deduced my lack of mathematical ability from that!'

He smiled, sadly. 'You know the popular saying that the three conditions impossible to conceal are a cough, wealth and being in love? Well, to me there is a fourth: mathematical gift.'

I laughed contemptuously. 'Oh, and you can no doubt identify it at a glance, eh? Is it a look in the eye or a certain *je ne sais quoi* that betrays to your ultra-fine sensibility the presence of mathematical genius? Can you perhaps also determine one's IQ with a hand-shake?'

'Actually there is an element of that "look in the eye",' he replied, ignoring my sarcasm. 'But in your case physiognomy was only a small part of it. The necessary – but not sufficient, mind you – precondition for supreme achievement is single-minded devotion. If you had the gift that you yourself would like to have had, dear boy, you wouldn't have come asking for my blessing to study mathematics; you would have gone ahead and done it. *That* was the first tell-tale sign!'

The more he explained himself, the angrier I got. 'If you were so certain I wasn't gifted, Uncle, why did you put me through the horrific experience of that summer? Why did I have to be subjected to the totally unnecessary humiliation of thinking myself a near-idiot?'

'But, don't you see?' he answered merrily. 'Goldbach's Conjecture was my security! If by some remote chance I'd been wrong about you and, in the most unlikely instance, you were indeed earmarked for greatness, then the experience wouldn't have crushed you. In fact it would not have been at all "horrific", as you significantly termed it, but exciting and inspiring and invigorating. I gave you an ultimate trial of determination, you see: if, after failing to solve the problem I'd set you – as, of course, I knew you would – you came back eager to learn more, to persist in your attempt for better or for worse, then I'd see you might have it in you to become a mathematician. But you . . . you weren't even curious enough to ask the solution! Indeed, you even gave me a signed declaration of your incompetence!'

The pent-up anger of many years now exploded. 'Do you know something, you old bastard? You may once have been a good mathematician, but as a human being you rate zero! Absolutely, totally *zilch!*'

To my surprise, this opinion was rewarded with a huge, hearty smile. 'On that, most favoured of nephews, I couldn't agree with you more!'

A month later I returned to the United States to prepare for my Senior year. I now had a new room-mate, unrelated to mathematics. Sammy had meanwhile graduated and was at Princeton, already deeply involved in the problem that would in due course become his doctoral dissertation – with the exotic title: 'The orders of the torsion subgroups of Ω_n and the Adams spectral sequence'.

On my first free weekend I took the train and went to visit him. I found him quite changed, much more nervous and irritable than I had known him in the year of our association. He'd also acquired some kind of facial tic. Obviously, the torsion subgroups of Ω_n (whatever they were) had taken their toll on his nerves. We had dinner at a small pizza place across from the university and there I gave him a shortened version of Uncle Petros' story, as I'd heard it from him. He listened without once interrupting for question or comment.

After I was finished, he summed up his reaction in two words: 'Sour grapes.'

'What?'

'You should know – Aesop was a Greek.'

'What's Aesop got to do with it?'

'Everything. The fable of the fox who couldn't reach a yummy bunch of grapes and therefore decided they were unripe anyway. What a wonderful excuse your uncle found for his failure: he put the blame on Kurt Gödel! Wow!' Sammy burst out laughing. 'Audacious! Unheard of! But I have to grant it to him, it is original; in fact it's unique, it should go into some book of records! Never before has there been a mathematician seriously attributing his failure to find a proof to the Incompleteness Theorem!'

Although Sammy's words echoed my own first doubts, I lacked the mathematical knowledge to understand this immediate verdict.

'So, you think it's impossible that Goldbach's Conjecture is unprovable?'

'Man, what does "impossible" mean in this context?' Sammy sneered. 'As your uncle correctly told you, there is, thanks to Turing, no way of telling with certainty that a statement is *a priori* unprovable. But if mathematicians involved in advanced research started invoking Gödel, no one would ever go near the interesting problems – you see, in mathematics the interesting is always difficult. The Riemann Hypothesis has not yielded to proof after more than a century? A case of application of the Incompleteness Theorem! The Four Colour Problem? Likewise! Fermat's Last Theorem still unproved? Blame it on evil Kurt Gödel! No one would ever have touched Hilbert's Twenty-three Problems;* indeed it's conceivable that all mathematical research, except the most trivial, would come to an end. Abandoning the study of a particular problem because it *might* be unprovable is like . . . like . . .' His face lit up when he found the appropriate analogy. 'Why, it's like not

* The great unsolved problems stated by David Hilbert at the International Congress of Mathematicians in 1900. Some, like the Eighth Problem (the Riemann Hypothesis) are still outstanding, but in others there has been progress and a few have been completely solved – as, for example, the Fifth, proved by Gleason, Montgomery and Zippen; the Tenth, by Davis, Robinson and Matijasevic; the Fourteenth, proved false by Nagata; the Twenty-second, solved by Deligne.

going out in the street for fear that a brick might fall on your head and kill you!'

'Let's face it,' he concluded, 'your Uncle Petros simply and plainly *failed* to prove Goldbach's Conjecture, like many greater men before him. But because, unlike them, he had spent his whole creative life on the problem, admitting his failure was unbearable. So, he concocted for himself this far-fetched, extravagant justification.'

Sammy raised his soda-glass in a mock toast. 'Here's to far-fetched excuses,' he said. Then he added in a more serious tone: 'Obviously, for Hardy and Littlewood to have accepted him as a collaborator, your uncle must have been a gifted mathematician. He could have made a great success of his life. Instead, he wilfully chose to throw it away by setting himself an unattainable goal and going after a notoriously difficult problem. His sin was Pride: he presumed that he would succeed where Euler and Gauss had failed.'

I was laughing now.

'What's so funny?' asked Sammy.

'After all these years of grappling with the mystery of Uncle Petros,' I said, 'I'm back to square one. You just repeated my father's words, which I high-handedly rejected as philistine and coarse in my adolescence: "The secret of life, my son, is to set yourself attainable goals." It's exactly what you are saying now.

That he didn't do so is, indeed, the essence of Petros' tragedy!'

Sammy nodded. 'Appearances are after all deceptive,' he said with mock-solemnity. 'It turns out the wise elder in the Papachristos family is *not* your Uncle Petros!'

I slept on the floor of Sammy's room that night, to the familiar sound of his pen scratching on paper accompanied by the occasional sigh or groan, as he struggled to untangle himself from the knots of a difficult topological problem. He left early in the morning to attend a seminar and in the afternoon we met at the Mathematics Library at Fine Hall, as arranged.

'We are going sightseeing,' he said. 'I have a surprise for you.'

We walked a distance on a long suburban road lined with trees and strewn with yellow leaves.

'What courses are you taking this year?' Sammy asked as we walked towards our mysterious destination.

I started to list them: Introduction to Algebraic Geometry, Advanced Complex Analysis, Group Representation Theory . . .

'What about Number Theory?' he interrupted.

'No. Why do you ask?'

'Oh, I've been thinking about this business with

your uncle. I wouldn't want you getting any crazy ideas into your head about following family tradition and tackling –'

I laughed. '*Goldbach's Conjecture*? Not bloody likely!'

Sammy nodded. 'That's good. Because I have a suspicion that you Greeks are attracted to impossible problems.'

'Why? Do you know any others?'

'A famous topologist here, Professor Papakyriakopoulos. He's been struggling for years on end to prove the "Poincaré Conjecture" – it's the most famous problem in low-dimensional topology, unproved for more than sixty years . . . ultra-hyper-difficult!'

I shook my head. 'I wouldn't touch anybody's famous unproved ultra-hyper-difficult problem with a ten-foot pole,' I assured him.

'I'm relieved to hear it,' he said.

We had reached a large nondescript building with extensive grounds. Once we had entered, Sammy lowered his voice.

'I got a special permit to come, in your honour,' he said.

'What is this place?'

'You'll see.'

We walked down a corridor and entered a large, darkish room, with the atmosphere of a slightly shabby but genteel English gentlemen's club. About fifteen men, ranging from middle-aged to elderly, were seated in leather armchairs and couches, some by the windows, reading newspapers in the scanty daylight, others talking in little groups.

We settled ourselves at a little table in a corner.

'See that guy over there?' Sammy said in a low voice, pointing to an old Asian gentleman, quietly stirring his coffee.

'Yes?'

'He is a Nobel Prize in Physics. And that other one at the far end' – he indicated a plump, red-haired man gesturing heatedly as he spoke to his neighbour with a strong accent – 'is a Nobel Prize in Chemistry.' Then he directed my attention to two middle-aged men seated at a table near us. 'The one on the left is André Weil –'

'*The* André Weil?'

'Indeed, one of the greatest living mathematicians. And the other one with the pipe is Robert Oppenheimer – yes, *the* Robert Oppenheimer, the father of the atom bomb. He's the Director.'

'Director of what?'

'Of this place here. You are now in the Institute for Advanced Study, think-tank for the world's greatest scientific minds!'

I was about to ask more when Sammy cut me short. 'Shh! Look! Over there!'

A most odd-looking man had just come in through

the door. He was about sixty, of average height and emaciated to an extreme degree, wearing a heavy overcoat and a knitted cap pulled down over his ears. He stood for a moment and peered at the room vaguely through extremely thick glasses. No one paid him any attention: he was obviously a regular. He made his way slowly to the tea and coffee table without greeting anybody, filled a cup with plain boiling water from the kettle and made his way to a seat by a window. He slowly removed his heavy overcoat. Underneath it he was wearing a thick jacket over at least four or five layers of sweaters, visible through his collar.

'Who is that man?' I whispered.

'Take a guess!'

'I haven't the slightest idea – he looks like a street person. Is he mad, or what?'

Sammy giggled. 'That, my friend, is your uncle's nemesis, the man who gave him the pretext for abandoning his mathematical career, none other than the father of the Incompleteness Theorem, the great Kurt Gödel!'

I gasped in amazement. 'My God! *That's* Kurt Gödel? But, why is he dressed like that?'

'Apparently he is convinced – despite his doctors' total disagreement – that he has a very bad heart and that unless he insulates it from the cold with all those clothes it will go into arrest.'

'But it's warm in here!'

'The modern high priest of Logic, the new Aristotle, disagrees with your conclusion. Which of the two should I believe, you or him?'

On our walk back to the university Sammy expounded his theory: 'I think Gödel's insanity – for unquestionably he is in a certain sense insane – is the price he paid for coming too close to Truth in its absolute form. In some poem it says that "people cannot bear very much reality", or something like that. Think of the biblical Tree of Knowledge or the Prometheus of your mythology. People like him have surpassed the common measure; they've come to know more than is necessary to man, and for this hubris they have to pay.'

There was a wind blowing, lifting dead leaves in whirls around us. I sighed.

I'll cut a long story (my own) short:

I never did become a mathematician, and this not because of any further scheming by Uncle Petros. Although his 'intuitive' depreciation of my abilities had definitely played a part in the decision by nurturing a constant, nagging sense of self-doubt, the true reason was fear.

The examples of the mathematical *enfants terribles* mentioned in my uncle's narrative – Srinivasa Ramanujan, Alan Turing, Kurt Gödel and, last but not least, himself – had made me think twice about whether I was indeed equipped for mathematical greatness. These were men who at twenty-five years of age, or even less, had tackled and solved problems of inconceivable difficulty and momentous importance. In this I'd definitely taken after my uncle: I didn't want to become a mediocrity and end up 'a walking tragedy', to use his own words. Mathematics, Petros had taught me, is a field that acknowledges only its greatest; this particular kind of natural selection offers failure as the only alternative to glory. Yet, hopeful as I still was in my ignorance about my abilities, it wasn't professional failure that I feared.

It all started with the sorry sight of the father of the Incompleteness Theorem padded with layers of warm clothing, of the great Kurt Gödel as a pathetic, deranged old man sipping his hot water in total isolation in the lounge of the Institute for Advanced Study.

When I returned to my university from the visit to Sammy, I looked up the biographies of the great mathematicians who had played a part in my uncle's story. Of the six mentioned in his narrative only two, a mere third, had lived a personal life that could be considered more or less happy and these two, significantly, were comparatively speaking the lesser men of the six, Caratheodory and Littlewood. Hardy and Ramanujan had attempted suicide (Hardy twice), and Turing had succeeded in taking his own life. Gödel's sorry state I've already mentioned.* Adding Uncle Petros to the list made the statistics even grimmer. Even if I still admired the romantic courage and persistence of his youth, I couldn't say the same of the way he'd decided to waste the second part of his life. For the first time I saw him for what he had clearly been all along, a sad recluse, with no social life, no friends, no aspirations, killing his time with chess problems. His was definitely not a prototype of the fulfilled life.

Sammy's theory of hubris had haunted me ever since I'd heard it, and after my brief review of mathematical history I embraced it wholeheartedly. His words about the dangers of coming too close to Truth in its absolute form kept echoing in my mind. The proverbial 'mad mathematician' was more fact than fancy. I came increasingly to view the great practitioners of the Queen of Sciences as moths drawn towards an inhuman kind of light, brilliant but scorching and harsh. Some couldn't stand it for long, like Pascal and Newton, who abandoned mathematics for theology.

* Gödel subsequently ended his own life, in 1978, while being treated for urinary tract problems at the Princeton County Hospital. His method of suicide was, like his great theorem, highly original: he died of malnutrition, having refused all food for over a month, convinced that his doctors were trying to poison him.

Others had chosen haphazard, improvised ways out – Evariste Galois' mindless daring that led to his untimely death comes immediately to mind. Finally, some extraordinary minds had given way and broken down. Georg Cantor, the father of the Theory of Sets, led the latter part of his life in a lunatic asylum. Ramanujan, Hardy, Turing, Gödel and so many more were too enamoured of the brilliant light; they got too close, scorched their wings, fell and died.

In a short while I realized that even if I did have their gift (which, after listening to Uncle Petros' story, I began seriously to doubt) I definitely did not want to suffer their personal misery. Thus, with the Scylla of mediocrity on the one side and the Charybdis of insanity on the other, I decided to abandon ship. Although I did, come June, eventually get my BA in Mathematics, I had already applied for graduate studies in Business Economics, a field that does not traditionally provide material for tragedy.

Yet, I hasten to add, I've never regretted my years as a mathematical hopeful. Learning some real mathematics, even my tiny portion of it, has been for me the most invaluable lesson of life. Obviously, everyday problems can be handled perfectly well without knowledge of the Peano–Dedekind Axiomatic System, and mastery of the Classification of Finite Simple Groups is absolutely no guarantee of success in business. On the other hand, the non-mathematician cannot conceive of the joys that he's been denied. The amalgam of Truth and Beauty revealed through the understanding of an important theorem cannot be attained through any other human activity, unless it be (I wouldn't know) that of mystical religion. Even if my education was meagre, even if it meant no more than getting my toes wet on the beach of the immense ocean of mathematics, it has marked my life for ever, giving me a small taste of a higher world. Yes, it has made the existence of the Ideal slightly more believable, even tangible.

For this experience I am forever in Uncle Petros' debt: it's impossible I would have made the choice without him as my dubious role model.

My decision to abandon plans of a mathematical career came as a joyful surprise to my father (the poor man had fallen into deep despair during my last undergraduate years), a surprise made even happier when he learned I would be going to business school. When, having completed my graduate studies and military service, I joined him in the family business, his happiness was at last complete.

Despite this volte-face (or maybe because of it?) my relationship with Uncle Petros blossomed anew after I returned to Athens, every vestige of bitterness on my part totally dissipated. As I gradually settled down to the routines of work and family life, visiting him became a frequent habit, if not a necessity. Our contact was an invigorating antidote to the increasing grind of the real world. Seeing him helped me keep alive that part of the self that most people lose, or forget about, with adulthood – call it the Dreamer or the Wonderer or simply the Child Within. On the other hand, I never understood what my friendship offered him, if we exclude the companionship he claimed not to need.

We wouldn't talk all that much on my visits to Ekali, as we'd found a means of communication better suited to two ex-mathematicians: chess. Uncle Petros was an excellent teacher and soon I came to share his passion (though unfortunately not his talent) for the game.

In chess, I also had the first direct experience of him as a thinker. As he analysed for my benefit the classic great games, or the more recent contests of the world's best players, I was filled with admiration for the workings of his brilliant mind, its immediate grasp of the most complex problems, its analytical power, the flashes of insight. When he confronted the board his features became fixed in utter concentration, his gaze became sharp and penetrating. Logic and intuition, the instruments with which he'd pursued for two decades the most ambitious intellectual dream, sparkled in his deep-set blue eyes.

Once, I asked him why he had never entered official competition.

He shook his head. 'Why should I strive to become a mediocre professional when I can bask in my status as an exceptional amateur?' he said. 'Besides, most favoured of nephews, every life should progress according to its basic axioms and chess wasn't among mine – only mathematics.'

The first time I ventured to ask him again about his research (after the extensive account of his life he had given me, we'd never again mentioned anything mathematical, both of us apparently preferring to let our sleeping dogs lie) he immediately dismissed the matter.

'Let bygones be bygones and tell me what you see on the chessboard. It's a recent game between Petrosian and Spassky, a Sicilian Defence. White takes Knight to f4 ...'

More oblique attempts didn't work either. Uncle Petros would not be coaxed into another mathematical discussion – period. Whenever I attempted a direct mention it would always be: 'Let's stick to chess, shall we?'

His refusals, however, didn't make me give up.

My wish to draw him once again to the subject of his life's work was not fired by mere curiosity. Although it was a long time since I had any news of my old friend Sammy Epstein (last time I'd heard of him he was an assistant professor in California), I couldn't forget his explanation of Uncle Petros giving up his research. In fact, I'd come to invest it with great existential significance. The development of my own affair with mathematics had taught me an important lesson: one should be brutally honest with oneself about weaknesses, acknowledge them with courage and chart further course accordingly. For myself I had done this, but had Uncle Petros?

These were the facts: a) From an early age he had chosen to invest all his energy and time in an incredibly, but most probably *not* impossibly, difficult problem, a decision which I still continued to regard as basically noble; b) As might reasonably have been expected (by others, if not by himself) he had not achieved his goal; c) He had blamed his failure on the incompleteness of mathematics, deeming Goldbach's Conjecture unprovable.

Of this much I was now certain: the validity of his excuse had to be judged by the strict standards of the trade and, according to these, I accepted Sammy Epstein's opinion as final – a final verdict of unprovability *à la* Kurt Gödel is just *not* an acceptable conclusion of the attempt to prove a mathematical statement. My old friend's explanation was much closer to the point. It wasn't because of his 'bad luck' Uncle Petros hadn't managed to achieve his dream. The appeal to the Incompleteness Theorem was indeed a sophisticated form of 'sour grapes', meant only to shelter him from the truth.

With the passing of the years, I had learned to recognize the profound sadness that pervaded my uncle's life. His absorption in gardening, his kindly smiles or his brilliance as a chess player couldn't disguise the fact that he was a broken man. And the closer to him I got, the more I realized that the reason for his condition lay in his profound insincerity. Uncle Petros had lied to himself about the most crucial event in his life and this lie had become a cancerous growth that stifled his essence, eating away at the very roots of his psyche. His sin, indeed, had been Pride. And the pride was still there, nowhere more apparent than in his inability to come face to face with himself.

I've never been a religious man, yet I believe there is great underlying wisdom in the ritual of Absolution: Petros Papachristos, like every human being, deserved to end his life unburdened of unnecessary suffering. In his case, however, this had the necessary prerequisite of his admitting the *mea culpa* of his failure.

The context here not being religious, a priest could not do the job.

The only person fit to absolve Uncle Petros was I

myself, for only I had understood the essence of his transgression. (The pride inherent in my own assumption I did not realize until it was too late.) But how could I absolve him if he did not first confess? And how could I lead him to confession unless we started once again to talk mathematics, a thing he persistently refused to do?

In 1971, I found unexpected assistance in my task.

The military dictatorship that then ruled the country, in a campaign to appear as a benevolent patron of culture and science, proposed to award a 'Gold Medal of Excellence' to a number of rather obscure Greek scholars who had distinguished themselves abroad. The list was short, since most of the prospective honourees, forewarned of the impending distinction, had hastened to exclude themselves; but topmost in it was 'the great mathematician of international fame, Professor Petros Papachristos'.

My father and Uncle Anargyros, in a totally uncharacteristic frenzy of democratic passion, strove to convince him to turn down this dubious honour. Talk of 'that old fool becoming the junta's lackey', 'giving the colonels an alibi', etc., filled our business offices and family homes. At moments of greater honesty the two younger brothers (both old men, by now) confessed to a less noble motive: the traditional re-

luctance of the businessman to be too closely identi-
fied with one political faction for fear of what will
happen when another comes to power. Yet I, an experienced Papachristos family observer, could also dis-
cern a strong need for them to be proved right in their
negative evaluation of his life, also tinged with an
element of envy. Father's and Uncle Anargyros'
world-view had always been founded on the simple
premise that Uncle Petros was bad and they good, a
black-and-white cosmology that distinguished between the grasshoppers and the ants, the dilettantes
and 'responsible men'. It didn't sit at all well with
them that the country's official government, junta or
no junta, should honour 'one of life's failures', when
the only rewards they ever got for their labours
(labours, mind you, that also put food on *his* table)
were financial.

I, however, took a different position. Beyond my
belief that Uncle Petros deserved the honour (he did,
after all, rate some recognition of his life's work, even
if it came from the colonels) I had an ulterior motive.
So I went to Ekali and, exercising to the full my influence as 'most favoured of nephews', convinced him to
overcome his brothers' hypocritical appeals to democratic duty as well as his own misgivings and accept his
Gold Medal of Excellence.

The award ceremony – that 'ultimate familial disgrace', according to Uncle Anargyros the late-bloom-ing radical – was held in the main auditorium of the University of Athens. The Rector of the School of Physics and Mathematics, in his ceremonial robes, gave a short lecture on Uncle Petros' contribution to science. Predictably enough he referred almost exclusively to the Papachristos Method for the Solution of Differential Equations, which he lauded with elaborate rhetorical effusions. Still, I was agreeably surprised to hear him also make passing reference to Hardy and Littlewood and their 'appealing to our great fellow-countryman for assistance with their most difficult problems'. While all this was being propounded I stole side-glances at Uncle Petros and saw him blushing red with shame again and again, all the time retreating further into the throne-like, gilded armchair where they had him installed. The Prime Minister (the arch-dictator) then bestowed the Gold Medal of Excellence and afterwards there was a short reception, during which my poor uncle was required to pose for photographs with all the top brass of the junta. (I have to confess that at this stage of the ceremony I felt a slight dose of guilt about the defining role I had played in his acceptance of the honour.)

When it was all over, he asked me to go back home for some chess, 'for purposes of recovery'. We started a game. I was a good enough player by that time to offer him decent resistance but not so good as to hold his interest after the ordeal he'd been through.

'What did you think of that circus?' he asked me, finally looking up from the board.

'The award ceremony? Oh, it was a bit boring, but I'm still glad you went through with it. Tomorrow it will be in all the newspapers.'

'Yes,' he said, 'how the Papachristos Method for the Solution of Differential Equations is almost on a par with Einstein's Theory of Relativity and Heisenberg's Uncertainty Principle, one of the crowning achievements of twentieth-century science . . . How that fool of a Rector carried on! Did you notice, by the way,' he added with a sour smile, 'the pregnant silence following the "ooohs" and "aaahs" and "ts-ts-ts's" of admiration at my extreme youth when I made the "great discovery"? You could almost hear everybody wondering: But how did the honouree spend the *next* fifty-five years of his life?'

Any sign of self-pity on his part bothered me inordinately.

'You know, Uncle,' I provoked him, 'it's not anybody's fault but your own that people don't know of your work on Goldbach's Conjecture. How could they – you've never told! Had you ever written up a report of your research, things would be different.

The story of your quest itself would make a worth-while publication.'

'Yes,' he sneered, 'a full footnote in *Great Mathematical Failures of Our Century*.'

'Well,' I mused, 'science advances by failures as well as successes. And anyway, it was a good thing your work in differential equations was acknowledged. I was proud to hear our family name associated with something other than money.'

Unexpectedly, a bright smile on his face, Uncle Petros asked me: 'Do you know it?'

'Do I know what?'

'The Papachristos Method for the Solution of Differential Equations?'

I'd been taken completely unawares and answered without thinking: 'No, I don't.'

His smile went away: 'Well, I expect they don't teach it anymore . . .'

I felt an upsurge of excitement – this was the chance I was waiting for. Although I had, in fact, ascertained while at university that the Papachristos Method was no longer taught (the advent of electronic calculation had rendered it obsolete), I lied to him, and with great vehemence: '*Of course* they teach it, Uncle! It's just that I never took an elective in differential equations.'

'Get paper and pencil then, and I'll tell you about it!'

I held back a triumphant cry. It was precisely what

I'd hoped for when I had convinced him to accept the medal: that the honour might reawaken his mathematical vanity and rekindle his interest in his art, enough of it anyway to lure him into a discussion of Goldbach's Conjecture and beyond . . . to his real reason for abandoning it. Explaining to me the Papachristos Method was an excellent introduction.

I rushed to fetch paper and pencil before he changed his mind.

'You'll have to be a little patient,' he began. 'A lot of water has gone under the bridge since then. Let's see now,' he murmured and began to scribble. 'Let us assume we have a partial differential equation in the Clairaut form . . . there! We now take . . .'

I followed his scribbles and explanations for almost an hour. Although I couldn't completely follow the argument, I showed exaggerated appreciation at every step.

'It's absolutely brilliant, Uncle!' I cried when he'd finished.

'Nonsense.' He brushed my praise aside, but I could see this modesty was not totally sincere. 'Sheer calculation of the grocery-bill variety, not real mathematics!'

The moment I was waiting for had arrived. 'Then talk to me about real mathematics, Uncle Petros. Talk to me about your work on Goldbach's Conjecture!'

He shot me a sideways glance, cunning, inquisitive and at the same time tentative. I held my breath.

'And what, if I may ask, is the purpose of your interest, Mr Almost-Mathematician?'

I had planned my answer to this beforehand, so as to put him in an emotional impasse.

'You owe it to me, Uncle! If for nothing else, to compensate me for that summer of anguish in my sixteenth year, when I struggled for three months to prove it myself, floundering in my abysmal ignorance!'

He appeared to be considering this for a while, as if to make a point of not giving in all too easily. When he smiled I knew I had won.

'What exactly do you want to know about my work on Goldbach's Conjecture?'

I left Ekali after midnight with a copy of *An Introduction to Number Theory* by Hardy and Wright. (I had to prepare myself by learning 'some fundamentals', he'd said.) I should point out to the non-specialist that mathematical books cannot normally be enjoyed like novels, in bed, in the bathtub, sprawled in an easy chair, or perched on the commode. To 'read' here means to understand, and for that you normally need a hard surface, paper, pencil and quality time. Since I had no intention of becoming a number theorist at the

advanced age of thirty, I went through the Hardy–
Wright book with only moderate attention ('moderate' in mathematics is 'considerable' by any other
measure), without persisting on fully comprehend-
ing those details that resisted the initial assault. Even
so, and taking into account that the study of the book
was not my main occupation, it took me almost a
month.

When I returned to Ekali, Uncle Petros, bless his
soul, started to examine me as if I were a schoolchild.

'Have you read the whole book?'

'I have.'

'State Landau's Theorem.'

I did.

'Write out for me the proof of Euler's Theorem of the
φ-function, the extension of Fermat's Little Theorem.'

I took paper and pencil and proceeded to do so, as
best as I could.

'Now prove to me that the non-trivial zeros of the
Riemann Zeta Function have real part equal to ½!'

I burst out laughing and he did too.

'Oh no, you don't!' I said. 'Not again, Uncle Petros!
It's enough that you set me to prove Goldbach's Con-
jecture. Find somebody else to assign the Riemann
Hypothesis!'

In the following two and a half months we had our
ten 'Lessons on Goldbach's Conjecture', as he called

them. What transpired in them is down on paper, with dates and times. Since I was now moving steadily towards the fulfilment of my main aim (his coming face to face with the reason for abandoning his research), I thought I'd also attain a secondary goal while at it: I kept meticulous notes so that, after his death, I could publish a short account of his odyssey, perhaps an insignificant footnote to mathematical history, but still a worthy tribute to Uncle Petros – if not, alas, to his ultimate success, then certainly to his ingenuity and, more importantly, his dedication and single-minded persistence.

During the course of the lessons I witnessed an amazing metamorphosis. The mild, kindly, elderly gentleman I had known since my childhood, one easily mistaken for a retired civil servant, turned before my eyes into a man illuminated by a fierce intelligence and driven by an inner power of unfathomable depth. I'd caught small glimpses of this species of being before, during mathematical discussions with my old room-mate, Sammy Epstein, or even with Uncle Petros himself, when he sat before his chessboard. Listening to him unravel the mysteries of Number Theory, however, I experienced for the first and only time in my life the real thing. You didn't have to know mathematics to feel it. The sparkle in his eyes and an unspoken power emanating from his whole being were testimony enough. He was the absolute thorough-bred, pure unadulterated genius.

An unexpected fringe benefit was that the last remaining trace of ambivalence (apparently it had been there, dormant, all those years) regarding the wisdom of my decision to abandon mathematics was now dispelled. Watching my uncle do mathematics was enough to confirm it to the full. I was not made of the same mettle as he – this I realized now beyond the shadow of a doubt. Faced with the incarnation of what I definitely was *not*, I accepted at last the truth of the dictum: *Mathematicus nascitur non fit*. The true mathematician is born, not made. I had not been born a mathematician and it was just as well that I had given up.

The exact content of the ten lessons is not within the scope of our story and I won't even attempt to refer to it. What matters here is that by the eighth we had covered the course of the initial period of Uncle Petros' research on Goldbach's Conjecture, culminating in his brilliant Partitions Theorem, now named after the Austrian who rediscovered it; also his other main result, attributed to Ramanujan, Hardy and Little-wood. In the ninth lesson he explained to me as much as I could understand of his rationale for changing the course of his attack from the analytic to the algebraic.

For the next he had asked me to bring along two kilos of lima beans. In fact, he had initially asked for navy beans, but then corrected himself, smiling sheepishly: 'Actually make it lima, so I can see them better. I'm not getting any younger, most favoured of nephews.'

As I drove to Ekali for the tenth (which, although I didn't know it yet, would be the last) lesson, I felt apprehensive: I knew from his narrative that he had given up precisely while working with the 'famous bean method'. Very soon, even in that imminent lesson, we would be reaching the crucial point, his hearing of Gödel's Theorem and the end of his efforts to prove Goldbach's Conjecture. It would be then that I would have to launch my attack on his dearly held defences and expose his rationalization about unprovability for what it was: a mere excuse.

When I got to Ekali he led me without a word to his so-called living room, which I found transformed. He'd pushed back what furniture there was against the walls, including even the armchair and the small table with the chessboard, and piled even higher piles of books along the perimeter, to create a wide, empty area in the centre. Without so much as a word he took the bag from my hands and started to arrange the beans on the floor, in a number of rectangles. I watched silently.

When he had finished he said: 'During our previous lessons we went over my early approach to the

Conjecture. In this I had done good, perhaps even excellent, mathematics – but mathematics, nevertheless, of a rather traditional variety. The theorems I had proved were difficult and important, but they followed and extended lines of thought started by others, before me. Today, however, I will present to you my most important and original work, a groundbreaking advance. With the discovery of my geometric method I finally entered virgin, unexplored territory.'

'All the more pity that you abandoned it,' I said, preparing the climate from the start for a confrontation.

He disregarded this and continued: 'The basic premise behind the geometric approach is that multiplication is an unnatural operation.'

'What on earth do you mean by *unnatural*?' I asked.

'Leopold Kronecker once said: "Our dear God made the integers, everything else is the work of man." Well, in the same way he made the integers, I think Kronecker forgot to add, the Almighty created addition and subtraction, or *give and take*.'

I laughed. 'I thought I came here for lessons in mathematics, not theology!'

Again he continued, ignoring the interruption. 'Multiplication is unnatural in the same sense as addition is natural. It is a contrived, second-order concept, no more really than a series of additions of equal elements. 3 × 5, for example, is nothing more than 5+5+5. To invent a name for this repetition and call it an 'operation' is the devil's work more likely . . .'

I didn't risk another facetious comment.

'If multiplication is unnatural,' he continued, 'more so is the concept of "prime number" that springs directly from it. The extreme difficulty of the basic problems related to the primes is in fact a direct outcome of this. The reason there is no visible pattern in their distribution is that the very notion of multiplication – and thus of primes – is unnecessarily complex. This is the basic premise. My geometric method is motivated simply by the desire to construct a natural way of viewing the primes.'

Uncle Petros then pointed at what he'd made while he was talking. 'What is that?' he asked me.

'A rectangle made of beans,' I replied. 'Of 7 rows and 5 columns, their product giving us 35, the total number of beans in the rectangle. All right?'

He proceeded to explain how he was struck by an observation which, although totally elementary, seemed to him to have great intuitive depth. Namely, that if you constructed, in theory, all possible rectangles of dots (or beans) this would give you all the integers – except the primes. (Since a prime is never a product, it cannot be represented as a rectangle but only as a single row.) He went on to describe a calculus for operations among the rectangles and gave me some examples. Then he stated and proved some elementary theorems.

After a while I began to notice a change in his style. In our previous lessons he'd been the perfect teacher, varying the tempo of his exposition in inverse proportion to its difficulty, always making sure I had grasped one point before proceeding to the next. As he advanced deeper into the geometric approach, however, his answers became hurried, fragmented and incomplete to the point of total obscurity. In fact, after a certain point my questions were ignored and what might have appeared at first as explanations I recognized now as overheard fragments of his ongoing internal monologue.

At first, I thought this anomalous form of presentation was a result of his not remembering the details of the geometric approach as clearly as the more conventional mathematics of the analytic, and making desperate efforts to reconstruct it.

I sat back and watched him: he was walking about the living room, rearranging his rectangles, mumbling to himself, going to the mantelpiece where he'd left paper and pencil, scribbling, looking something up in a tattered notebook, mumbling some more, returning to his beans, looking here and there, pausing, thinking, doing some more rearranging, then scribbling some more . . . Increasingly, references to a 'promising line of thought', 'an extremely elegant lemma' or a 'deep little theorem' (all his own inventions, obviously) made his face light up with a self-satisfied smile and his eyes sparkle with boyish mischievousness. I suddenly realized that the apparent chaos was nothing else than the outer form of inner, bustling mental activity. Not only did he remember the 'famous bean method' perfectly well – its memory made him positively gloat with pride!

A previously unthought-of possibility quickly entered my mind, only to become a near conviction moments later.

When first discussing Uncle Petros' abandoning Goldbach's Conjecture with Sammy, it had seemed obvious to both of us that the reason was a form of burnout, an extreme case of scientific battle fatigue after years and years of fruitless attacks. The poor man had striven and striven and striven and, after failing each time, was finally too exhausted and too disappointed to continue, Kurt Gödel providing him with a convenient if far-fetched excuse. But now, watching his obvious exhilaration as he played around with his beans, a new and much more exciting scenario presented itself: was it possible that, in direct contrast to what I'd thought until then, his surrender had come at the very peak of his achievement? In fact, precisely at the point when he felt he was *ready to solve* the problem?

In a flash of memory, the words he had used when describing the period just before Turing's visit came back – words whose real significance I had barely realized when I'd first heard them. Certainly he'd said that the despair and self-doubts he had felt in Cambridge, in that spring of 1933, had been stronger than ever. But had he not interpreted these as the 'inevitable anguish before the final triumph', even as the 'onset of the labour pains leading to the delivery of the great discovery'? And what about what he'd said a little earlier, just a little while ago, about this being his 'most important work', 'important and original work, a groundbreaking advance'? Oh my good God! Fatigue and disillusionment didn't have to be the causes: his surrender could have been the loss of nerve before the great leap into the unknown and his final triumph!

The excitement caused by this realization was such that I could no longer wait for the tactically correct moment. I launched my attack right away.

'I notice,' I said, my tone accusing rather than observing, 'that you seem to think very highly of the "famous Papachristos bean method".'

I had interrupted his train of thought and it took a

few moments for my comment to register.

'You have an amazing command of the obvious,' he said rudely. 'Of course I think highly of it.'

'. . . in contrast to Hardy and Littlewood,' I added, delivering my first serious blow.

This brought the expected reaction – only to a much greater degree than I'd foreseen.

'"Can't prove Goldbach with beans, old chap!"' he said in a gruff, boorish tone, obviously parodying Littlewood. Then, he took on the other member of the immortal mathematical pair in a cruel mimicry of effeminacy. '"Too elementary for your own good, my dear fellow, infantile even!"'

He banged his fist on the mantelpiece, furious. 'That ass Hardy,' he shouted, 'calling my geometric method "infantile" – as if he understood the first thing about it!'

'Now, now, Uncle,' I said scoldingly, 'you can't go calling G. H. Hardy an ass!'

He banged his fist again, with greater force.

'An ass he was, and a sodomite too! The "great G. H. Hardy" – the Queen of Number Theory!'

This was so untypical of him I gasped. 'My, my, we are getting nasty, Uncle Petros!'

'Not at all! I'll call a spade a spade and a bugger a bugger!'

If I was startled I was also exhilarated: a totally new

man had magically appeared before my eyes. Could it be that, together with the 'famous bean method', his old (I mean his *young*) self had at last resurfaced? Could I now be hearing, for the first time, Petros Papachristos' real voice? Eccentricity – even obsession – was certainly more characteristic of the single-minded, over-ambitious, brilliant mathematician of his youth than the gentle, civilized manners I'd come to associate with my elderly Uncle Petros. Conceit and malice towards his peers could well be the necessary other side of his genius. After all, both were perfectly suited to his capital sin, as diagnosed by Sammy: Pride.

To push it to its limit I used a casual tone: 'G. H. Hardy's sexual inclinations do not concern me,' I said. 'All that is relevant, *vis-à-vis* his opinion of your "bean method", is that he was a great mathematician!'

Uncle Petros' face went crimson. 'Bollocks,' he growled. 'Prove it!'

'I don't have to,' I said dismissively. 'His theorems speak for themselves.'

'Oh? Which one?'

I stated two or three of the results I remembered from his textbook.

'Ha!' Uncle Petros snarled. 'Mere calculations of the grocery-bill variety! But show me one great idea, one

– 189 –

inspired insight . . . You can't? That's because there isn't one!' He was fuming now. 'Oh, and while you're at it, tell me of a theorem the old pansy proved on his own, without good old Littlewood or poor dear Ramanujan holding his hand – or whatever other part of his anatomy it was they were holding!'

The mounting nastiness signalled that we were approaching a breakthrough. A tiny extra bit of annoyance was probably all that was necessary to bring it about.

'Really, Uncle,' I said, trying to sound as haughty as possible. 'This is beneath you. After all, whatever theorems Hardy proved, they were certainly more important than yours!'

'Oh yes?' he snapped back. 'More important than *Goldbach's Conjecture*?'

I burst into incredulous laughter, despite myself. 'But you didn't *prove* Goldbach's Conjecture, Uncle Petros!'

'I didn't prove it, but –'

He broke off in mid-sentence. His expression betrayed he'd said more than he wanted to.

'You didn't prove it but *what*?' I pressed him. 'Come on, Uncle, complete what you were going to say! You didn't prove it but *were very close to it*? I'm right – am I not?'

Suddenly, he stared at me as if he were Hamlet and I

his father's ghost. It was now or never. I leapt up from my seat.

'Oh, for God's sake, Uncle,' I cried. 'I'm not my father or Uncle Anargyros or grandfather Papachristos! I know some mathematics, remember? Don't give *me* that crap about Gödel and the Incompleteness Theorem! Do you think I swallowed for a single moment that fairy tale of your "intuition telling you the Conjecture was unprovable"! No – I knew it from the very start for what it was, a pathetic excuse for your failure. *Sour grapes!*'

His mouth opened in wonder – from ghost I must have been transformed into a celestial vision.

'I know the whole truth, Uncle Petros,' I continued fervently. 'You got to within a hair's breadth of the proof! You were almost there . . . Almost . . . All but the final step . . .' – my voice was coming out in a humming, deep chant – '. . . and then, you lost your nerve! You chickened out, Uncle dearest, didn't you? What happened! Did you run out of willpower or were you just too scared to follow the path to its ultimate conclusion? Whatever the case, you'd always known it deep inside: the fault is *not* with the Incompleteness of Mathematics!'

My last words had made him recoil and I thought I might as well play the part to the hilt: I grabbed him by the shoulders and shouted straight into his face.

'Face it, Uncle! You owe it to yourself, can't you see that? To your courage, to your brilliance, to all those long, fruitless, lonely years! The blame for not proving Goldbach's Conjecture is all your own – just as the triumph would have been totally yours if you'd succeeded! But you didn't succeed! Goldbach's Conjecture *is* provable and you knew that all along! It's just that *you* didn't manage to prove it! You failed – you *failed*, God damn it, and you've got to admit it, at last!'

I had run out of breath.

As for Uncle Petros, for a slight moment his eyes closed and he wavered. I thought that he was going to pass out, but no – he instantly came to, his inner turmoil now unexpectedly melting into a soft, mellow smile.

I smiled too: naïvely, I thought that my wild ranting had miraculously achieved its purpose. In fact, at that moment I would have made a bet that his next words would be something like: 'You are absolutely right. I failed. I admit it. Thank you for helping me do it, most favoured of nephews. Now, I can die happy.'

Alas, what he actually said was: 'Will you be a good boy and go get me five more kilos of beans?'

I was stunned – all of a sudden he was the ghost and I Hamlet.

'We – we must finish our discussion first,' I faltered, too shocked for anything stronger.

But then he started pleading: 'Please! Please, please, *please* get me some more beans!'

His tone was so intolerably pathetic that my defences crumbled to dust. For better or for worse, I knew that my experiment in enforced self-confrontation had ended.

Buying uncooked beans in a country where people don't do their grocery shopping in the middle of the night was a worthy challenge to my developing entrepreneurial skills. I drove from taverna to taverna, beguiling the cooks into selling me from their pantry stock a kilo here, half a kilo there, until I accumulated the required quantity. (It was probably the most expensive five kilos of beans ever.)

When I got back to Ekali, it was past midnight. I found Uncle Petros waiting for me at the garden gate.

'You are late!' was his only greeting.

I could see that he was in a state of tremendous agitation.

'Everything all right, Uncle?'

'Are these the beans?'

'They are, but what's the matter? What are you so worked up about?'

Without answering he grabbed the bag. 'Thank

you,' he said and began to close the gate.

'Shan't I come in?' I asked, surprised.

'It's too late,' he said.

I was reluctant to leave him until I found out what was going on.

'We don't have to talk mathematics,' I said. 'We can have a little game of chess or, even better, drink some herbal tea and gossip about the family.'

'No,' he said with finality. 'Goodnight.' He walked fast towards his small house.

'When is the next lesson?' I shouted after him.

'I'll call you,' he said, went in and banged the door behind him.

I remained standing on the pavement for a while, wondering what to do, whether to attempt once again to enter the house, to talk to him, to see if he was all right. But I knew he could be stubborn as a mule. Anyway, our lesson and my nocturnal search for beans had drained me of all energy.

Driving back to Athens I was pestered by my conscience. For the first time, I questioned my course of action. Could my high-handed stance, supposedly intended to lead Uncle Petros into a therapeutic showdown, have been nothing more than my own need to get even, an attempt to avenge the trauma he'd inflicted on my teenage self? And, even if that weren't so, what right did I have to make the poor old man face

the phantoms of his past, despite himself? Had I seriously considered the consequences of my inexcusable
immaturity? The unanswered questions abounded,
but still, by the time I got home I had rationalized
myself out of the moral tight spot: the distress I'd obviously caused Uncle Petros had most probably been the
necessary – the obligatory – step in the process of his
redemption. What I'd told him was, after all, too much
to digest at one go. Obviously the poor man only
needed a chance to think things over in peace. He had
to admit his failure to himself, before he could do so to
me . . .

But if that was the case, why the extra five kilos of
beans?

A hypothesis had begun to form in my mind, but it
was too outrageous to be given serious consideration
– until morning anyway.

Nothing in this world is truly new – certainly not the
high dramas of the human spirit. Even when one
such appears to be an original, on closer examination
you realize it's been enacted before, with different
protagonists, of course, and quite possibly with
many variations in its development. But the main
argument, the basic premise, repeats the same old
story.

The drama played out during Petros Papachristos'

final days is the last in a triad of episodes from the history of mathematics, unified by a single theme: the Mystery-solution to a Famous Problem by an Important Mathematician.[*]

By majority consent, the three most famous unsolved mathematical problems are: (a) Fermat's Last Theorem, (b) the Riemann Hypothesis and (c) Goldbach's Conjecture.

In the case of Fermat's Last Theorem, the mystery-solution existed from its first statement: in 1637, while he was studying Diophantus' *Arithmetica*, Pierre de Fermat made a note in the margin of his personal copy, right next to proposition II.8 referring to the Pythagorean theorem, in the form $x^2 + y^2 = z^2$. He wrote: 'It is impossible to separate a cube into two cubes, or a biquadrate (fourth power) into two biquadrates, or generally any power except a square into two powers with the same exponent. I have discovered a truly marvellous proof of this, which, however, this margin is not large enough to contain.'

After the death of Fermat his son collected and published his notes. A thorough search of his papers, however, failed to reveal the *demonstratio mirabilis*, the 'marvellous proof' that his father claimed to have found. Equally in vain have mathematicians ever

[*] Mystery-solutions to famous problems by charlatans are two-a-penny.

since sought to rediscover it.* As for the verdict of history on the existence of the mystery-solution: it's ambiguous. Most mathematicians today doubt that Fermat indeed had a proof. The worst-case theory has it that he was consciously lying, that he had not verified his guess and his margin-note was mere bragging. What's likelier, however, is that he was mistaken, the *demonstratio mirabilis* crippled by an undetected fault.

In the case of the Riemann Hypothesis, the mystery-solution was in fact a metaphysical practical joke, with G. H. Hardy as its perpetrator. This is how it happened:

Preparing to board a cross-Channel ferry during a bad storm, the confirmed atheist Hardy sent off to a colleague a postcard with the message: 'I have the proof to the Riemann Hypothesis.' His reasoning was that the Almighty, whose sworn enemy he was, would not permit him to reap such an exalted undeserved reward and would therefore see to his safe arrival, in order to have the falsity of his claim exposed.

---

* Fermat's Last Theorem was, amazingly, proved in 1993. Gerhard Frey first proposed that the problem could possibly be reduced to an unproven hypothesis in the theory of elliptic curves, called the Taniyama–Shimura Conjecture, an insight later conclusively proven by Ken Ribet. The crucial proof of the Taniyama–Shimura Conjecture itself (and thus, as its corollary, Fermat's Last Theorem) was achieved by Andrew Wiles; in the final stage of his work he collaborated with Richard Taylor.

The mystery-solution of Goldbach's Conjecture completes the triad.

On the morning after our last lesson, I telephoned Uncle Petros. At my insistence, he had recently agreed to have a line installed, on the condition that only I, and no one else, would know the number.

He answered sounding tense and distant. 'What do you want?'

'Oh, I just called to say hello,' I said. 'Also to apologize. I think I was unnecessarily rude last night.'

There was a pause.

'Well,' he said, 'actually I'm busy at the moment. Why don't we talk again . . . shall we say next week?'

I wanted to assume that his coldness was due to the fact that he was upset with me (as he had every reason to be, after all) and merely expressing his resentment. Still, I felt a nagging unease.

'Busy with what, Uncle?' I persisted.

Another pause.

'I-I'll tell you about it some other time.'

He was obviously eager to hang up so, before he could cut me off, I impulsively blurted out the suspicion that had taken shape during the night.

'You wouldn't by any chance have resumed your researches, would you, Uncle Petros?'

I heard a sharp intake of breath. 'Who – who told you that?' he said hoarsely.

I tried to sound casual. 'Oh, come on, give me some credit for having come to know you. As if it needed telling!'

I heard the click of his hanging up. My God – I was right! The crazy old fool had gone off his rocker. He was trying to prove Goldbach's Conjecture!

My guilty conscience stung me. What had I done? Humankind indeed cannot stand very much reality – Sammy's theory of Kurt Gödel's insanity also applied, in a different way, to Uncle Petros. I had obviously pushed the poor old man to his uttermost limit and then beyond it. I'd aimed straight at his Achilles heel and hit it. My ridiculous simple-minded scheme to force him into self-confrontation had destroyed his fragile defences. Heedlessly, irresponsibly, I had robbed him of the carefully nurtured justification of his failure: the Incompleteness Theorem. But I had put nothing in its place to sustain his shattered self-image. As his extreme reaction now showed, the exposure of his failure (to himself, more than to me) had been more than he could bear. Stripped of his cherished excuse he had taken, of necessity, the only way left for him to go: madness. For what else was the endeavour to search, in his late seventies, for the proof that he had failed to find when he was at the peak of his powers? If that wasn't total irrationality, what was?

I walked into my father's office filled with apprehension. Much as I hated to allow him into the charmed circle of my bond with Uncle Petros, I felt obliged to let him know what had happened. He was after all his brother, and any suspicion of serious illness was certainly a family matter. My father dismissed my self-recriminations about causing the crisis as so much poppycock. According to the official Papachristos world-view, a man had only himself to blame for his psychological condition, the only acceptable external reason for emotional discomfort being a serious drop in the price of stocks. As far as he was concerned, his older brother's behaviour had always been bizarre, and one more instance of eccentricity was definitely not to be taken seriously.

'In fact,' he said, 'the condition you describe – absent-mindedness, self-absorption, abrupt changes of mood, irrational demands for beans in the middle of the night, nervous tics, etc. – reminds me of how he was carrying on when we visited him in Munich, back in the late twenties. Then, too, he was behaving like a madman. We'd be at a nice restaurant enjoying our *wurst* and he'd be squirming around as if there were nails in his chair, his face twitching like mad.'

'*Quod erat demonstrandum,*' I said. 'That's exactly it. He's back doing mathematics. In fact, he's back working on Goldbach's Conjecture – ridiculous as that may sound at his age.'

My father shrugged. 'It's ridiculous at any age,' he said. 'But why worry? Goldbach's Conjecture has already done him all the harm possible. Nothing worse can come of it.'

But I wasn't so sure about that. In fact, I was quite certain that a lot worse things could be in store for us. Goldbach's resurrection was bound to stir up unfulfilled passions, to aggravate deep-buried, terrible, unhealed wounds. His absurd new application to the old problem boded no good.

After work that evening, I drove to Ekali. The ancient VW beetle was parked outside the house. I crossed the front yard and rang the bell. There was no response, so I shouted: 'Open up, Uncle Petros; it's me!'

For a few moments I feared the worst, but then he appeared at a window and stared vaguely in my direction. There was no sign of his usual pleasure at seeing me, no surprise, no greeting – he just stared.

'Good afternoon,' I said. 'I just came by to say hello.'

His normally serene face, the face of a stranger to life's usual worries, was now marked by extreme tension, his skin pale, his eyes red with sleeplessness, his brow furrowed with concern. He was also unshaven, the first time I'd seen him so. His stare continued absent, unfocused. I wasn't even sure he knew who I was.

'Come on, Uncle dear, please open up for the most favoured,' I said with a fatuous smile.

He disappeared and after a while the door creaked open. He stood there, blocking my entry, wearing his pyjama bottoms and a wrinkled vest. It was evident he didn't want me to enter.

'What's wrong, Uncle?' I asked. 'I'm worried about you.'

'Why should you be worried?' he said, now forcing himself to sound normal. 'Everything's fine.'

'Are you sure?'

'Of course I'm sure.'

Then, with a snappy gesture, he beckoned me closer. After quickly, anxiously glancing around, he leaned towards me, his lips almost touching my ear, and whispered: 'I saw them again.'

I didn't understand. 'Who did you see?'

'The girls! The twins, the number 2^{100}!'

I remembered the strange apparitions of his dreams.

'Well,' I said, trying to sound as casual as possible. 'If you are once again involved with mathematical research, you are once again having mathematical dreams. Nothing strange about that . . .'

I wanted to keep him talking so as to (figuratively, but if need be also literally) put a foot in the door. I had to get some sense of how bad his condition was.

'So what happened, Uncle,' I asked, feigning great

interest in the matter. 'Did the girls speak to you?'

'Yes,' he said, 'they gave me a . . .' His voice quickly trailed off, as if he was afraid he'd said too much.

'A what?' I asked. 'A clue?'

He became suspicious again. 'You mustn't tell,' he said sternly.

'Mum's the word,' I said.

He had started to close the door. Convinced now that his situation was extremely serious and that the time had come for emergency action, I grasped the knob and started to push. As he felt my force, he tensed up, gritted his teeth and struggled to prevent me from entering, his face contorted to a grimace of desperation. Fearing the effort might be too much for him (he was nearing eighty, after all) I reduced the pressure a bit for a final attempt at reason.

Of all the possible stupid things I could have said to him, I chose this: 'Remember Kurt Gödel, Uncle Petros! Remember the Incompleteness Theorem – Goldbach's Conjecture is unprovable!'

Instantly, his expression changed from despair to wrath. 'Fuck Kurt Gödel,' he barked, 'and fuck his Incompleteness Theorem!' With an unexpected upsurge of strength, he overcame my resistance and slammed the door shut in my face.

I rang the bell again and again, banged the door with my fist and shouted. I tried threats, reasoning and pleading, but nothing worked. When a torrential October rain began to fall I hoped that, mad or not, Uncle Petros might be moved by mercy and let me in. But he wasn't. I left, soaking wet and very worried.

From Ekali I drove straight to our family doctor and explained the situation. Without altogether ruling out serious mental disturbance (possibly triggered by my unwarranted interference in his defence mechanisms) he suggested two or three organic problems as likelier causes of my uncle's transformation. We decided to go to his house first thing the next morning, force our way in if necessary, and submit him to a thorough medical examination.

That night I couldn't sleep. The rain was getting stronger, it was past two o'clock and I was sitting at home hunched in front of the chessboard, just as Uncle Petros must have been on innumerable sleepless nights, studying a game from the recent world championship. Yet my concern kept interfering and I couldn't concentrate.

When I heard the ringing I knew it was he, even though he'd never yet initiated a call on his newly installed telephone.

I jumped up and answered.

'Is that you, Nephew?' He was obviously all worked up about something.

'Of course it's me, Uncle. What's wrong?'

'You must send me someone. Now!'

I was alarmed. '"Someone"? A *doctor* you mean?'

'What use would a doctor be? A mathematician, of course!'

I humoured him: 'I'm a mathematician, Uncle; I'll come right away! Just promise to open the door, so I won't catch pneumonia and –'

He obviously didn't have time for irrelevancies. 'Oh hell!' he grunted and then: 'All right, all right, you come, but bring another one as well!'

'Another *mathematician*?'

'Yes! I must have two witnesses! Hurry!'

'But why do the witnesses have to be mathematicians?'

Naively, I had thought at first he wanted to write his will.

'To understand my proof!'

'Proof of *what*?'

'Goldbach's Conjecture, you idiot – what else!'

I chose my next words very carefully. 'Look, Uncle Petros,' I said, 'I promise to be with you as soon as my car will get me there. Let's be reasonable, mathematicians aren't kept on call – how on earth can I get one at two o'clock in the morning? You'll tell me all about your proof tonight and tomorrow we will go together –'

But he cut me off, screaming. 'No, no, no! There's no time for any of that! I need my two witnesses and I need them *now*!' Then he broke down and started sobbing. 'O nephew, it's so ... it's so ...'

'So *what*, Uncle? Tell me!'

'Oh, it's so simple, so *simple*, my dearest boy! How is it possible that all those years, those endless years, I hadn't realized how blessedly simple it was!'

I cut him off. 'I'll be there as soon as I can.'

'Wait! Wait! Waaaaa-it!!!' He was now in panic. 'Swear you won't come alone! Get the other witness! Hurry . . . Hurry up, I implore you! Get the witness! There's no time!'

I tried to appease him: 'Oh, come on, Uncle; there can't be such a rush. The proof won't go away, you know!'

These were his last words: 'You don't understand, dear boy – there's no time left!' His voice then dropped to a low, conspiratorial whisper, as if he didn't want to be overheard by someone close by: 'You see, the girls are here. They are waiting to take me.'

By the time I arrived in Ekali, breaking all speed records, it was too late. Our family doctor (I had picked him up on the way) and I found Uncle Petros' lifeless body slumped on the paving of his little terrace. The torso was leaning against the wall, the legs spread open, the head turned towards us as if in welcome. A flash of distant lightning revealed his features fixed in a wonderful smile of deep, absolute contentment – I imagine it was that which guided the doctor in his instant diagnosis of a stroke. All around him were hundreds of lima beans. The rain had destroyed their neat parallelograms and now they were scattered all over the wet terrace, sparkling like precious jewels.

The rain had just stopped and the air was infused with the invigorating smell of wet earth and pine trees.

Our last exchange over the telephone is the only evidence of Petros Papachristos' mystery-solution to Goldbach's Conjecture.

Unlike Pierre de Fermat's illustrious marginal note, however, it is extremely unlikely that my uncle's *demonstratio mirabilis* of his famous problem will tempt a host of mathematical hopefuls to attempt to reproduce it. (No rise in the price of beans is expected.) This is as it should be. Fermat's sanity was never in question; no one ever had reason to believe he was in anything less than total possession of his senses when he stated his Last Theorem. Unfortunately, the same cannot be said of my Uncle Petros. When he announced his triumph to me he was probably as mad as a hatter. His last words were uttered in a state of terminal confusion, the total relinquishment of logic, the Night of Reason that dimmed the light of his final moments. It would thus be extremely unfair to have him posthumously declared a charlatan by attributing a serious intention to a declaration obviously made in a half-delirious state, his brain most probably already ravaged by the stroke that, a short while later, killed him.

So: did Petros Papachristos prove Goldbach's Conjecture in his final moments? The wish to protect his memory from any chance of ridicule obliges me to state it as unequivocally as possible: the official answer must be 'No'. (My own opinion need not concern mathematical history – I will therefore keep it to myself.)

The funeral was strictly family, with only a wreath and a single representative from the Hellenic Mathematical Society.

The epitaph later carved on Petros Papachristos' tomb, below the dates marking the limits of his earthly existence, was chosen by me, after I had overcome the initial objections of the family elders. They form one further addition to the collection of posthumous messages that make the First Cemetery of Athens one of the world's most poetic:

EVERY EVEN NUMBER GREATER THAN 2
IS THE SUM OF TWO PRIMES

Post Scriptum

At the time this book was completed, Goldbach's Conjecture was two hundred and fifty years old. To this day it remains unproven.

Acknowledgements

I wish to thank Professors Ken Ribet and Keith Conrad, who carefully read the revised manuscript and corrected numerous mistakes, as well as Dr Kevin Buzzard for the clarification of various points – obviously, any remaining mathematical flaws are my own. Also my sister, Cali Doxiadis, for her invaluable linguistic and editorial advice.

APOSTOLOS DOXIADIS

A Note on the Author

Apostolos Doxiadis received a Bachelor's Degree in Mathematics from Columbia University in New York and a Master's Degree in Applied Mathematics from the École Pratique des Hautes Etudes in Paris. He has run a number of successful computer companies, as well as written and directed for both the screen and the stage. The second of his two feature films, *Tetriem*, won the prize of the International Center for Artistic Cinema at the 1988 Berlin International Film Festival. Apostolos Doxiadis lives in Athens, Greece.